CUPCAKES FOR MY ORC ENEMY

FAIRHAVEN FALLS

HONEY PHILLIPS

To Louise
thanks for reading!
love, ♡
Honey

 Created with Vellum

CHAPTER 1

*E*lara eased her new pink smart car into the parking space on Main Street with a relieved sigh. After ten years of living in the city, she'd forgotten whatever parallel parking skills she might have once had. The small car was the perfect choice—it didn't even take up an entire parking space. True, getting here through the mountains had been a little nerve-racking, but she had no intention of making the trip on a frequent basis.

She pushed the button to turn off the car and looked around happily. Fairhaven Falls was as perfect as it had appeared in the brochures the Town Council had sent her. The wide main road leading down to the river was lined with small independent shops. A row of connected two-story buildings lined her side of the street, each of them sporting different colors and slightly different styles. The other side of the street was a mixture of larger buildings and converted houses, gradually becoming more residential as the road rose up into the mountains that surrounded the town.

Wreaths hung from the old-fashioned gas lamp posts lining the street, but they too were an eclectic mix, ranging from a bright pink one with what looked like tiny white skulls to a plain pine wreath on the post in front of the store next to hers. Whoever had put it up hadn't even gone to the trouble of tying a bow on it and she shook her head. Some people obviously didn't have the town spirit. *Some people...*

Her thoughts stuttered to a halt as a couple came strolling up the sidewalk. They were wearing matching L.L. Bean flannel shirts and jeans, holding hands and smiling at each other like any happy couple—except he was a minotaur, complete with brown fur, massive horns, and very large hooves. His companion was... She wasn't exactly sure about the female, but given the catlike eyes and pointed ears, not to mention blue hair that was clearly not dyed, his partner clearly wasn't human.

I knew what I was getting into, she reminded herself, and gave the couple a friendly wave. The man nodded, dipping his horns, while the girl returned her wave and she relaxed. It wasn't as if she hadn't seen the Others before, but they were far scarcer in the city. They tended to gravitate towards the smaller towns, sometimes to the point where there were very few humans left. Which was why she was here—as part of the effort by the Town Council to attract more humans to Fairhaven Falls and keep the town growing and thriving.

They had discussed the matter in depth on one of their many Zoom calls. The mayor was also a minotaur, but seeing him on the small screen of the computer was not quite the same as having a seven-foot male stomping by, his footsteps shaking her small car.

But this was the right thing to do, she was sure of it. Last year had been the worst year of her life. She had decided to change everything, from her job to her home, and Fairhaven Falls was her new start. Today was the first day of her new life.

She carefully adjusted her blue knit hat and matching scarf and climbed out of the car. The big windows of her new coffee shop were covered with brown paper, white canvas draped across the sign above. There was a large poster on one of the windows, and she gave it an approving nod. The Winter Festival it advertised was the result of one of the discussions she'd had with the Council. Monthly seasonal events designed to attract visitors. Not only would they be good for business, but with any luck they would also attract new residents.

The poster was designed to mimic a vintage advertising poster complete with a stylized picture of a snow-covered Main Street and an extremely hunky yeti on skis. Everything about it screamed winter fun... except that the weather was not at all wintry. There was no snow in town and only a faint dusting of white at the very top of the surrounding mountains. In fact, her scarf and hat were already starting to feel a little too warm with the sun beating down on her back. As attractive as the town looked, without snow it would be a disappointment for anyone expecting a more traditional seasonal setting.

Still pondering the situation, she moved to the door of her new shop and pulled out the old-fashioned brass key. The door of the store next to hers was identical, and there was a delicious aroma wafting from it. The display cases in the front window were filled with the most delicious baked goods she'd ever seen, although they had not been arranged with any degree of artistry. A few decorative platters, maybe a raised cake stand or two, and some accessories would definitely elevate the display. She'd have to suggest it when she met the owner, but in the meantime she was dying to see her own shop. So far she'd only seen it on camera, and she couldn't wait to see it in person.

She stepped inside and took a deep, satisfied breath. She could already smell the scent of coffee from the beans that had been delivered the previous day. The wall to the left had been stripped back to reveal the weathered brick soaring up to the twelve-foot ceiling. Comfortable chairs and couches in a mixture of fabrics and sizes were scattered artfully around the room, along with a number of tables. She was pleased to see that two of the smaller tables had been arranged in the bay window, a perfect spot to drink coffee and gaze out over the town.

Large blackboards in ornate wooden frames were hung on the back wall, ready to display the daily specials. The counters gleamed in dark slate, the refrigerated cases beneath them ready to be filled with an assortment of goods from an organic bakery in California. Although even online they hadn't looked anywhere near as enticing as the goods next door.

The undoubted star of the place was the gleaming brass and steel Italian coffee maker that dominated the rear counter. It had cost almost as much as her car, but it was definitely going to be worth it. In fact, she couldn't wait to try it out. She opened a bag of medium roast Brazilian arabica and made herself an espresso with the ease of long practice. She had made her way through college working as a barista and her skills hadn't left her.

As she sipped her coffee, a muffled roar came from the bakery next door, and she frowned at the dividing wall. The two stores had once been a single unit, and the wall between them was wood rather than brick. She'd covered it with white shiplap and hung some of her own pictures on it, hoping to eventually turn it into a gallery of local works. But even though she was pleased with the aesthetics, she hoped there wasn't going to be a lot of disruption from next door. Still, she had an excellent sound system, and she could always turn it up a little if necessary.

Behind the main shop was an industrial chic bathroom and a big storage room lined with wooden shelves. The closed door next to them concealed the staircase leading to her upstairs apartment, but she bypassed it in favor of inspecting her new kitchen. The exposed brick continued in here as well, along with gleaming metal work surfaces and a weathered wooden table. Rustic wooden shelves contained a miscellaneous collection of mugs.

A door in the back wall let out onto the old loading dock and alley, but it was nothing like a city alley. A paved parking area separated the building from a narrow lane still paved in the original cobbles. A mixture of residential and commercial back yards lined the other side of the lane, and it was a surprisingly charming space. She gave the paved parking area a thoughtful look. Perhaps she could turn it into an outdoor seating area when spring arrived. She might have to add a wall to create a path past the kitchen, but she had a small amount left in her budget.

And maybe I can even do some of the work myself.

Not that she knew anything about construction, of course, but you could learn almost anything from YouTube videos. She hummed happily and returned to the kitchen. A basket on the kitchen table contained a welcome message from the Council, a bottle of wine, a cardboard container of frozen soup, and a plate of obviously homemade cookies. She opened the wine and poured some into a *Kiss the Librarian* coffee mug, then went to explore the upstairs.

5

The apartment over the store also had an exposed brick wall, wooden floors, and big windows. Unfortunately, it contained almost nothing else. In her determination to start over, she had given away all of her furniture. There were a few cardboard boxes full of the possessions she couldn't bear to part with, her clothes, a box containing an air mattress, and almost nothing else. Damn. She'd ordered a few pieces of furniture, but they were already late and she wasn't sure how long it would take for them to arrive.

Thank goodness she had also ordered the air mattress. She tugged the surprisingly heavy box into the back room she intended to use as her bedroom and opened it, only to discover that there was no pump included. Sitting down on the floor next to it, she gave it a try, but after twenty minutes and a rapidly developing headache, she abandoned the effort. She would just have to make do until she could find a pump.

She wandered back downstairs and realized that the container of soup hadn't even begun to thaw. She put it in the microwave on low and went back into the shop to study it thoughtfully. She was pleased with her furniture choices, but they definitely needed a little rearranging to form the cozy little nooks she had in mind. She refilled her wine mug and set to work. She started pushing the furniture around, imagining a college student working diligently here, a group of women chatting on the chaises, and a courting couple in the two big wingback chairs. She was bending over a coffee table, trying to push it into place, when a loud roar made her jump.

"What the hell do you think you're doing?"

She whirled around to find a very large, very angry orc glaring at her.

CHAPTER 2

"*W*ell?" Grondar snapped. "What do you want?"

The human male in front of the counter took another step back, wringing his hands nervously.

"It's just that it all looks so good," the man mumbled.

Fuck. He despised humans, and he despised humans who wasted his time even more. He was on the verge of ordering the man to leave when the door opened and Ermengarde came rushing in. As usual she was dressed all in black, but her bright pink hair and cheerful smile were the complete opposite of her goth style—not to mention her sparkly pink wings.

"You're late," he growled.

"Sorry, boss. Eldegar was in trouble at school again, and I had to stop by and smooth things over."

With the help of a little pixie dust, no doubt. But considering that Ermengarde was the oldest of six children, all of them as mischievous as only pixies could be, he couldn't really blame her.

She slipped behind the counter, pulled on her apron—black, of course—and smiled at the human.

"How can I help you?"

The man gave her a besotted look, and Grondar grunted and escaped to the sanctuary of his kitchen. He pulled out the ingredients for a new recipe he wanted to try and was soon lost in the familiar routine. His grandmother had taught him to cook when he came to live with her after his parents died, and the solace he'd found then had never left him.

"You've got to stop scaring away the customers, boss," Ermengarde said cheerfully as she came into the kitchen and hopped up on the counter, her wings fluttering.

"Get down from there. It's not sanitary," he ordered. "I just wanted him to make up his fucking mind."

"Then you shouldn't make everything taste so good." She grinned at him and stole one of his new cookies. "Oh my God, this is so good. What is it?"

"Almond flour. Cranberries. Walnuts."

She rolled her eyes.

"Does it have a name?"

"It doesn't need a name."

"Whatever. I'll add them to the display case, okay?"

He frowned at her.

"I'm not sure they're right yet."

"They're perfect, and you know it." She gave him a speculative glance from under her lashes. "Did you know that the grand opening for the shop next door is happening on Friday?"

"No, and I don't care," he snapped.

She held up her hands in mock apology and grabbed the tray of cookies.

"I'll just put these in the display case. Don't forget the order of cupcakes for Mrs. Harrison's kindergarten class."

"I never forget an order."

Ermengarde grinned and left, her wings fluttering. He brought out the tray of cupcakes he'd already baked and set to work on the icing. But his previous serenity had vanished and he found himself scowling at the wall separating his bakery from the shop next door. He'd really wanted the space to expand his own store—and he'd been prepared to pay well for it—but the Town Council had refused his offer. They hadn't explained why, just that they had other plans for the space.

The place had been under construction for the past two months and there had been a number of deliveries, but he refused to pay any attention to what they were doing. He'd shut down any speculation about it in his presence so firmly that no one had the nerve to bring up the subject any more.

It doesn't matter. He'd just focus on his own business and wait for the new shop to fail. The odds were in his favor—Fairhaven Falls was a small town, and new businesses frequently struggled to find customers. The knowledge helped calm him, and he concentrated on the cupcake order.

He had finished the cupcakes and was onto a batch of cookies when he suddenly smelled smoke. Puzzled, he checked his ovens, but everything was working normally. Then he noticed a white haze drifting down from the edge of the ceiling. The store next door. *Fuck.*

Reaching for his phone, he raced out his kitchen door and tried the corresponding kitchen door. To his surprise, it wasn't locked and he hurried in. Greasy black smoke poured out of a microwave. He swore again and pulled the door open to reveal the smoldering remains of one of Wu Ling's takeout containers. He grabbed a set of tongs and dumped it into the metal sink, pouring water over it. A quick glance at the rest of the kitchen revealed no other flames, just a smoky haze, and he decided it wasn't worth calling the fire department.

The new owner must have arrived. What kind of idiot put metal in a microwave? He heard a muffled grunt from the shop at the front of the building and stomped down the hallway to find out.

A female was bent over one of the ridiculous pieces of furniture that now cluttered the space—a female with the most perfect ass he'd ever seen, lush enough for even his big hands. His shaft stiffened at the thought, irritating him even more. He had no use for females, no matter how tempting.

Frustration made his tone even more hostile.

"What the hell do you think you're doing?"

She gasped, straightening up and whirling around. A human. *Fuck.* She was ridiculously small—the top of her head wouldn't even reach his chest—but absolutely everything he liked had been packed onto her small frame. Lush breasts, a softly curved waist, and that ass that practically begged for his touch. Her blonde hair was up in a high ponytail, perfect for wrapping around his hand as he—

Fuck! He pushed the image away as fast as he could, even though his shaft was already straining painfully against his jeans. She was human and he had no use for humans.

Disappointment made him growl at her again.

"Are you trying to set my shop on fire?"

CHAPTER 3

*E*lara stared up at the orc. He was easily as tall as the minotaur, but instead of fur, he had smooth, dark green skin covering broad shoulders, bulging arms, and an impressively muscled chest—all of which she could see clearly since only a white apron covered that wide chest. His dark hair was piled on top of his head in a messy bun, and equally dark eyes blazed at her from a rugged, masculine face. Two sharp white tusks framed a surprisingly sensuous mouth and her gaze snagged on them. *How did you kiss someone with tusks*, she thought, then blushed at the thought.

"Are you trying to set my shop on fire?"

"I'm sorry, what?"

She finally managed to tear her gaze away from his mouth only to find he was still glaring at her. He gave an impatient grunt, grabbed her arm, and tugged her back down the hallway. The huge hand clasped around her arm was surprisingly gentle, but absolutely inescapable despite her protests. The objections died when they ended up in the kitchen—a kitchen now filled with smoke. The smoldering remains of the container that had held her soup were in the big metal sink, and she gave them a horrified look.

"I don't understand. What happened?"

He pointed at the blackened microwave, black marks streaking up the wall behind it.

"Why did that happen? It was just a paper container."

"A paper container with a metallic dragon on the side. Everyone in town knows you can't use Wong Li's containers in the microwave," he growled.

"Well, I'm not from town so I didn't know," she said indignantly. "How did you get in here anyway?"

"Through the back door. The door you left unlocked."

His frown intensified, and she was suddenly very aware of the fact that he was still holding her arm. Their bodies were only inches apart, and she could feel the heat radiating from his, heat and a delicious spicy scent.

She took a deep breath, trying to catch more of that delectable scent, and as she did, the tips of her breasts brushed against his very hard chest. A heated spark of arousal flared between them, and she gasped. His hand tightened on her arm before he dropped it and took two big steps back.

He turned on the fan over the big industrial stove, then turned and stomped back to the front of the shop. She followed. His back, left bare by the apron, was just as impressive as his chest, but her gaze snagged on his butt. He was wearing faded jeans beneath the apron, and the worn cloth clung lovingly to a truly magnificent ass.

Her nipples throbbed, and she brought up her arm to cover them just as he snatched open the front door and turned around to glare at her. His eyes dropped to where her arm was positioned across her breasts, and she actually saw him swallow hard. Maybe he wasn't quite as infuriated by her as he appeared.

He snatched his gaze away, looking around at the rest of the room, then frowned again.

"What is this place?"

"My coffee shop."

"There is no need for a coffee shop in Fairhaven Falls," he growled.

"I don't understand. The Town Council was very enthusiastic about my proposal. I didn't think the town already had a coffee—"

"They do. And I own it."

Why hadn't the Town Council mentioned that? The last thing she wanted was to compete with a business owned by a local resident. Maybe there was a way for them to spread out the business.

"What kind of coffees do you make?" she asked cautiously.

"Real coffee." He scowled. "Although I keep a thermos of decaf for anyone who can't handle the real thing."

Real coffee? That was his idea of a coffee shop? She did her best not to laugh.

"So you don't make espressos or lattes or anything like that?"

"No," he said shortly, and she smiled at him.

"Then I don't think it will be a problem. I make specialty coffees. It's completely different."

"Fucking Town Council," he muttered. "I assume this was their idea?"

"Yes and no. I presented them with a couple of different ideas, but we all liked this one the most. They thought a coffee shop would appeal to the locals, as well as be a selling point for new residents, and they didn't want to bring in a chain."

He didn't seem to be listening. If anything he was scowling even more ferociously—and why did he look so hot while he was doing it? He took a step closer and her heart began to pound, but she refused to step back.

"I don't understand. Why are you so angry? It's just coffee."

"Because I wanted this space in order to expand my business," he snapped.

The pieces suddenly clicked into place.

"Oh, I didn't realize. Of course. You must own the bakery next door. I'm Elara. I'm very happy to meet you."

"Are you, Elara?" His voice turned low and dangerous. "Is that why you're already trying to sabotage me by burning down my bakery?"

"I wasn't trying to sabotage you," she said indignantly. "But if I was, you couldn't stop me."

She immediately regretted the impulsive words as his eyes narrowed and he bent down towards her.

"Maybe not, but I'll make sure you regret it."

"Oh yeah? How?"

For all his bluster, she didn't think he'd hurt her.

"Don't think for one moment that I'd hesitate to pull you over my knee and spank that luscious little ass of yours."

Oh my.

Her mouth suddenly went dry, and she licked her lips nervously. That dark gaze immediately focused on her mouth as he took another step closer to her. Her heart was beating even wilder, but it wasn't from fear. Time slowed to a crawl as their eyes locked—and then he was gone again.

"Close the doors as soon as the air clears. Make sure you lock them this time," he ordered, and stomped back down the hallway.

Her knees threatened to give way, and she collapsed into the nearest chair, an old wooden rocking chair, and stared at the empty hallway. He was the biggest, most obnoxious male she'd ever met in her life—and she'd never been so turned on. She usually preferred charming, conventionally handsome men, even if her choices hadn't worked out particularly well up to now. She certainly wasn't interested in an enormous bad-tempered male, no matter what her body thought. She would just have to stay as far away from him as possible.

CHAPTER 4

ighting down the urge to make sure that Elara was obeying his orders, Grondar stomped back into his kitchen. His grandmother was there, perched on the stool he kept for that purpose. At some point in the past, one of his ancestors had mated a fairy and some trick of genetics had resulted in his grandmother being half the size of a normal orc female—although she more than made up for it in personality.

She was busily stirring raisins into a batch of scone dough—a batch he had intended to keep raisin free. As usual she was dressed in one of the colorful sweatsuits she favored, but he'd never seen this one before.

"Do you know you have the word Juicy written across your ass?"

"You watch your language, boy."

Since he knew she could outswear a river nymph, the rebuke didn't bother him. The fact that she twisted an inch of skin between her strong little fingers did.

"That hurts."

"It's supposed to. Where have you been? It's not like you to leave in the middle of the day. I don't suppose you slipped away for a little afternoon delight?"

Elara's pretty face immediately appeared in his mind, and he scowled.

"Of course not."

She sighed. "I thought it was too much to hope for. You'd be a lot more agreeable if you'd just get laid."

"Gran!"

"Don't look so shocked. We both know you need a good f—"

"I'm not discussing this with you."

His ears burned with embarrassment, but to his relief she let the subject drop.

"Then where were you?"

"Next door. Making sure the new owner didn't burn the place down."

"Fireworks already?"

She started to cackle, and he glared at her.

"Why the hell did you bring in a human?"

"It will be good for the town. Just wait and see. Now help me down."

He lifted her off the stool, and she gave his cheek a quick kiss.

"Now get back to work."

"Yes, ma'am."

"Good boy."

She grinned at him and swished her Juicy-covered ass out of the kitchen. He looked at the bowl of dough and sighed. As much as he hated to admit it, the raisins would be a nice accent to the orange flavors in the dough. He set to work rolling it out, doing his best not to think about his annoying new neighbor.

It didn't work. She kept popping up in his mind as he worked. As he closed the shop and mopped the floors, he kept thinking of the way her ponytail bounced when she walked and the tempting sway of her ass. As he cleaned the kitchen, making sure that everything was pristine and ready for the morning, he remembered those sparkling blue eyes and the lush curve of her mouth.

When he finally turned out the lights and left, he couldn't help glancing next door. The downstairs was in darkness, but the lights were on in the apartment above the shop. She must be living there. Even as he thought that, she appeared in the window of the room over the kitchen—the completely uncovered window. She was no longer wearing the fuzzy white sweater that had clung so delightfully to her abundant breasts. Instead, she was wearing something pink and silky with tiny straps that revealed her luscious cleavage.

He growled, even as his shaft stood up and took notice. Did the woman have no sense at all? Standing in front of a lighted window wearing practically nothing? He glared down the alley. It didn't get a lot of traffic, but it was far from unused. Anyone walking along it would only have to glance up to see her there. *Fuck.* He stomped across to her back door and turned the handle. Thank the gods she'd at least had the sense to lock it. Instead, he pounded on it with his fist. A moment later, he heard footsteps.

"Who is it?"

"Grondar."

"Who?"

She sounded puzzled, but she still unlocked the door and opened it.

"Woman, do you have no sense of self-preservation?" he asked, crowding his way inside.

She looked up at him, her eyes wide, and he realized that her outfit was even better—or worse—than he suspected. The silky pink garment skimmed tantalizingly over her curves and barely reached her thighs. She'd pulled on a matching pink robe, but it was open down the front and barely longer than the nightgown.

"What's the matter? What did I do now?"

"You don't have any curtains," he growled, taking a step closer. She gulped and backed up a step.

"I know. I haven't had a chance to get them yet."

"Which means that anyone looking up from the alley can see you. All of you."

He took another step towards her, and she backed away again, but now her back was against the wall and she couldn't escape him. Her cheeks flushed, but she gave him a defiant look.

"I didn't think anybody would be looking. And it's not as if I'm naked."

The vision of her naked body pressed to the glass immediately popped into his head, and he groaned. Her eyes widened again, and then that soft pink mouth curved into a smile.

"Are you disappointed?"

"Elara..." he growled, warning her.

"I guess it's a good thing you weren't there a few minutes earlier when I got out of my bath."

For the first time, he noticed that her hair was pulled up on her head, damp tendrils curling at the base of her neck and her skin flushed and glowing.

"You changed clothes in front of an uncovered window? Do you enjoy flaunting yourself?"

The teasing look vanished, replaced by an entirely too adorable attempt to look fierce.

"I was not flaunting myself."

She actually stomped her foot, and for some reason that pushed him over the edge. He grabbed the soft curve of her waist, hauled her up the wall until their heads were on the same level, and then he kissed her. As soon as their lips touched, he froze. *What the hell am I doing?*

He started to pull away, to mumble an apology, but then she sighed against his mouth and kissed him back. Her luscious mouth was perfectly positioned between his tusks as her lips parted and the smallest, most seductive tongue he'd ever encountered slid into his mouth. He groaned again, and took over, forcing her lips further apart so he could explore every delicious inch. She tasted like wine and cookies and something that was uniquely her, and he was instantly addicted to her taste.

He pulled her closer, one hand reaching down to cover that glorious silk covered ass. His fingers dug into the soft flesh, and she moaned into his mouth. He squeezed her ass again, delighting in her responsiveness, and she writhed against him.

The sound of a car grumbling down the alley over the cobblestones finally penetrated the haze of lust. He recognized it as the ancient Cadillac belonging to Gladys Cravets, one of his grandmother's closest friends, and suddenly realized he was mauling Elara in front of the still open door. He immediately dropped her to her feet and stepped back. She put her hands against the wall as if she needed the support and looked up at him, her eyes wide and midnight blue. Her mouth was red and swollen, and he could see her big nipples tenting the pink silk.

He knew he should apologize, but how could he when that had been the best kiss of his entire life? And with a human. *Fuck.*

"Lock the door behind me," he ordered. "And stay away from those damn windows."

He stomped out of the door towards his truck, but he didn't get in until he heard the door close and the lock click into place. Then he climbed in, started the engine, and drove to the end of the alley. He didn't pull out onto the road along the river, watching in the rearview mirror until he saw her windows go dark. Even then, he remained hunched over the steering wheel as he replayed the last moments over and over in his head.

It can never happen again.

He would just have to stay as far away from her as he could. And really, how hard could it be? He was sure they had absolutely nothing in common.

CHAPTER 5

*C*lara walked into the kitchen and winced at the sunlight streaming in through the uncovered window. After Grondar's lecture, she'd ended up spending the night on one of the couches in the coffee shop. It was comfortable enough, but it wasn't designed for sleeping. Instead, she'd moodily watched videos, finished up the bottle of wine, and tried unsuccessfully not to think about her grumpy neighbor.

Why did he have to be such a good kisser? She couldn't remember ever getting so turned on so fast before. She would have been totally embarrassed about her reaction to him if he hadn't kissed her back with equal hunger. When he put her down, she'd brushed against the front of his body, and it was very, very clear that he was just as aroused.

The memory of that massive erection haunted her, and when the wine kicked in and she finally fell into a restless sleep, she had some very explicit dreams. So explicit that she blushed when she looked at the big wooden table in the kitchen. In her dream, he hadn't stopped with a kiss, and she'd ended up spread out on the kitchen table instead.

It was just a dream. A ridiculous dream.

She had better things to do than mooning over the big, grouchy male. Her stomach rumbled in seeming agreement and she sighed. Because of the soup disaster, she hadn't had anything for dinner the previous evening except for cookies. She opened the big refrigerator, then sighed again. No food. There should be a delivery coming later today, but that didn't help her now.

Still, it was as good a reason as any to go out and see more of the town. She hurried upstairs to dig through her boxes of clothing. Thank goodness they'd made it. She settled on a baby blue turtleneck and dark wash skinny jeans, then went to wash and change in the tiny old fashioned bathroom. Although she didn't really believe that anyone could see her, especially if she stayed away from the windows, she didn't want Grondar yelling at her again.

Unless it's followed by him kissing me.

Shaking her head at her foolishness, she pulled on her cute black ankle boots and headed back downstairs. The air outside was cool, but definitely not cold, and she gave the poster advertising the Winter Festival a worried look as she walked down the street towards the river. Most of the businesses weren't open yet, but almost all of them sported one of the posters.

She passed a werewolf in a flannel shirt who gave her a cheerful greeting and a slightly terrifying toothy smile. After her first moment of shock, she returned the greeting. Everyone else she passed also wished her a good morning. So different from the city, and so pleasant. It only confirmed her decision to move to Fairhaven Falls.

As she approached the river, the other side of the street opened out into the big town square. She gave it a quick glance, but she was more interested in the bustle of activity around the café on the corner. It had big windows overlooking the square and more overlooking the river, along with a broad deck. It would be a delightful spot when the weather was warmer, although a few brave souls were enjoying the sunshine. She blinked twice at a yeti in a pair of shorts, wondering if he was the one on the poster.

As she entered the café, the delicious smell of bacon made her mouth water but every table was occupied, including all the seats at the counter. The customers looked like any other small town customers—except for the flash of fur or fangs or even scales, but she did her best not to stare.

"Afraid you'll have to wait, sweetie."

An older waitress in a classic pink diner uniform smiled at her as she hurried past. The pink made a striking contrast to her pale blue skin and the silvery blue hair braided neatly around her head. Based on the delicious aromas filling the restaurant, it would be worth waiting, but she also had to get back in time for the deliveries she was expecting today. Before she could make up her mind, a tiny green-skinned female in a bright purple sweatsuit waved at her.

"Over here, Elara. Come and join us."

With a relieved sigh, she recognized Flora, one of the councilmembers whom she'd spoken to on Zoom, and went to join her. Flora was sharing a booth with a plump, older woman with a friendly face—and a witch's hat perched on top of her tight silver curls.

"Elara, this is Gladys Cravets. Her rear garden backs up to the alley behind your shop."

Gladys studied her with sharp blue eyes, and Elara suddenly found herself blushing, although she wasn't quite sure why. Then the woman grinned and patted the seat next to her.

"Sit down. I'm sure you must be hungry. Is your kitchen all right?"

She winced as she sat down.

"You know about that?"

Flora shrugged. "It's a small town. Word gets around. I already called Brian—he's the contractor who did most of the work on your building—and asked him to send someone over. I told him to bring you a new microwave and touch up the paint."

Flora's knowledge of the needed repairs was oddly specific. Did the councilmember have some sort of psychic powers? Her confusion must have shown on her face, because Flora laughed.

"No, I can't read your mind. My grandson told me about it."

"Grandson?"

"Grondar. The baker next door," she added when Elara's mouth dropped open. "Grumpy outside, marshmallow inside."

Marshmallow?!

"I knew who Grondar is," she said, and heard Gladys snicker. "He's your *grandson?*"

Flora had the same deep green skin but was even smaller than Elara—how could she possibly have ended up with such a giant grandson?

The other woman flashed her a grin.

"It doesn't seem possible, does it? My great-grandfather married a fairy, and apparently I inherited her size."

"And was Grondar's grandfather smaller as well?" she couldn't help asking.

"Oh no. He was large even for an orc." Flora laughed at her expression and winked. "Just because I'm small doesn't mean I don't appreciate a big co—"

"Gran! Do not finish that sentence."

That deep, gravelly voice was already way too familiar. She peeked up and saw Grondar frowning at the older woman. The frown deepened when he saw her looking at him—and why was he so damn hot when he was frowning? The mouth that had kissed her so passionately the night before was now pressed in a tight line, but it didn't stop her from staring at it and remembering. She jumped when Gladys cackled.

"You worked late last night, Grondar. I saw your... truck when I was coming home from the coven meeting."

Oh, Lord. From the meaningful pause and the gleeful tone in the witch's voice, Elara suspected she'd seen a lot more than Grondar's truck. She knew she was blushing again, but there was absolutely nothing she could do about it. From the twinkle in Flora's eyes, she guessed that Flora had already heard about it.

"Are you going to join us?" Flora asked.

"No. I have work to do. The fu—damn kitchen still smells like smoke."

Guilt immediately swamped her.

"I'm really sorry about that. Is there anything I can do to help?"

"Just stay away from my shop," he growled, bending down to glare at her.

He was looming over her exactly the same way he had done the previous night, and she licked her lips nervously. His gaze immediately focused on her mouth, and for a terrifying—and exhilarating—second she thought he was about to kiss her again in front of everyone in the café. Instead, he only grunted and straightened.

"I'll get my order to go."

He stomped away, and yes, his ass looked just as good today as it had the day before. She wasn't the only one to watch. A woman with short silvery fur actually leaned back in her chair in order to get a better look, and Elara had the oddest impulse to demand that she keep her eyes to herself. She forced herself to drag her eyes away and found Flora and Gladys exchanging meaningful looks.

The waitress dashed by, dropping off a mug of surprisingly good coffee.

"Your order will be ready in a minute," she said as she hurried away.

"What order? I didn't order anything."

Flora grinned at her. "Trust Rona. She'll bring you exactly what you want."

She had a sudden vision of the waitress returning with Grondar in tow, and she blushed again. Dammit. She was an intelligent, professional woman. She should not be reacting like a schoolgirl. Determined to remember her professional status, she brought up the subject of the Winter Festival.

"I noticed that almost all the stores are displaying the posters for the festival. Has there been much traffic on the website?"

Flora nodded happily. "Oh, yes. Dave says we're getting lots of views."

She was delighted that the campaign was working so well, but it only increased her worry.

"This was a brilliant idea, Elara," Flora continued. "Assuming it does well, we plan to have more of these events throughout the year."

"I'm afraid there's just one little problem. There's no snow."

Gladys gave her a puzzled look. "That's one of the advantages of living in the South. We have these spells of mild weather, even in the middle of winter."

"I'm sure it's very pleasant, but this is supposed to be a winter festival—complete with snow."

Flora pursed her lips, then nodded thoughtfully.

"It would make it difficult for some of the activities we had planned."

"We have two more weeks. Maybe it will snow by then?"

"It might." Flora tapped her fingers thoughtfully on the table, then looked over at Gladys. "Do you think we could increase that possibility?"

"Now, Flora, you know how much effort that takes. And a full coven. We only had five members show up last night for the new moon ritual and book club."

"Just tell me who was missing. I'll be happy to remind them that we all thrive when the town thrives."

Flora gave a fierce grin, and for the first time Elara noticed that her teeth were extremely sharp.

Gladys sighed. "If we have the full coven, we could give it a try. It might make a nice change from dancing around naked."

Elara ignored the naked comment and frowned at the witch.

"Wait a minute. Are you saying you can make it snow?"

Gladys tried to look modest and failed. "I believe so."

Elara stared at her for a moment then gave a delighted laugh.

"That would be wonderful. If we have snow, then we could still have the snow castle contest and the ice carving exhibition."

Flora gave her an approving smile just as the waitress placed a plate in front of Elara. A thick piece of what looked like home-made bread covered with a generous layer of perfectly ripened avocado topped by a poached egg and accompanied by three strips of bacon, extra crispy. Flora had been right—Rona had brought her exactly what she wanted. She turned to thank the waitress, but she was already gone. Instead, she smiled at Flora and Gladys.

"I'm going to love living here."

CHAPTER 6

*M*ore annoying eighties pop drifted through the wall of his shop, and Grondar scowled. It didn't help that several of the customers waiting in line were bobbing their heads in time to the music. Scowling, he turned to the ancient CD player that he kept behind the counter to listen to when he was cleaning up at night and slammed in a disc.

The heavy bass thundered out of the speakers, drowning out her catchy little song, and he grinned in satisfaction. Then the lyrics began and old Mrs. Jasper gasped. He winced as he realized he had inadvertently grabbed an old Nine Inch Nails CD.

"Sorry about that!" he yelled as he tried desperately to shut off the machine. In his haste, he only succeeded in making it louder, and with a frustrated roar he slammed the machine to the ground.

A heavy silence fell, and he turned around to find all his customers staring at him.

"Sorry," he began again just as the door swung open and a cute little blonde head appeared.

"Is everything all right? We heard a crash."

"Equipment malfunction," he growled.

"Oh." Her eyes sparkled with mischief. "Your music did seem a little... ambitious for this time of day. Maybe you should save it for the evening."

She smiled at him in what he was sure was a deliberately provocative gesture, and he could all too clearly envision doing just what the lyrics promised. He had taken two steps towards her before he regained control. She raised an eyebrow, then grinned again and left, her ponytail bobbing provocatively behind her.

He was fighting the urge to go after her when the door opened again and Ermengarde returned from her lunch break. He immediately focused on the white cup she was carrying—a white cup with a jaunty little logo spelling out Java Joy, complete with a heart replacing the O.

"What is that?" he demanded.

The pixie just grinned.

"It's called a Speckled Owl, and it's marvelous."

"A Speckled Owl? What the hell is that?"

"Let me see if I remember. Oh, yes, it's a latte with hazelnut, vanilla, and nutmeg. And speckles of happiness," she added with a mischievous smile.

"Happiness? Are you fucking kidding me?"

"Nope. That's exactly what it says on the menu board."

Ermengarde grinned again as she pulled on her apron and joined him behind the counter, bringing the wretched substitute for actual coffee with her. It was just as well she hadn't been delayed today. As much as he hated to admit it, in the three days since the coffee shop had opened, his business had been busier than ever.

"You know I don't want you bringing that crap in here," he growled and snatched the cup away from her, but she only smiled at him.

"That's all right. I've already finished most of it anyway."

She turned to the next customer, one of the members of Mrs. Cravets's coven, who was listening eagerly.

Great. That no doubt meant he'd be getting another visit from his grandmother to lecture him about the businesses in town supporting each other. He'd heard it the first time when he refused to attend the grand opening of the coffee shop, and at least once a day since then.

He stomped back into the kitchen and was about to throw away the remnants of what was clearly not coffee when he hesitated. After a quick glance to make sure that he was really alone, he opened the lid and took a sip. *Oh, fuck.* The rich bitterness of the coffee was expertly layered with the creaminess of the vanilla and hazelnut, the nutmeg striking the perfect note. It was absolutely delicious.

But it doesn't make me happy, he told himself as he finished the regrettably small amount left in the cup, crumpled the cup, and tossed it in the trash. *It would make you happy if Elara were serving it to you, preferably naked,* a wicked inner voice taunted him, and he slammed his hands down on the counter.

"Everything all right back there, boss?" Ermengarde called.

"Fine," he growled as he began pulling ingredients to make cupcakes.

But it wasn't fine. It had not been fine since the utterly frustrating—and utterly tempting—female had moved in next door. He was doing his best to ignore her, but it was almost impossible. He would walk into the River Café and see her ponytail swinging as she huddled with his grandmother and her cronies. He would decide to go for a walk and she would be ahead of him on the sidewalk, that spectacular ass moving in a way that seemed calculated to mesmerize him.

She'd even parked her ridiculous pink car much too close to his big green truck—so close that he actually picked it up and moved it away, setting off the alarm in the process. Lights came on up and down the alley, and she peeked out at him behind the sheets that now regrettably covered her windows. Her mouth formed a perfect O of astonishment, and he had a sudden vision of sliding his cock between those pretty pink lips.

Then she gave him a teasing, provocative smile, and he had to clamp his hand down on the side of his truck to stop himself from finding out exactly what she meant by that smile. The fact that he dented his truck in the process only made him more annoyed.

No. He was not going to think about her. He concentrated on his baking and had just finished putting together the batter when the back door opened and the frustrating female walked in.

She was wearing loose jeans and an oversized flannel shirt with the sleeves pushed up. Her face was flushed, the short hairs around her face curling wildly. She had flour on her cheek and down her shirt and still looked as tempting as ever.

"Oh, that smells good." Her small nose twitched. "Coffee and hazelnut. Maybe vanilla and something else? What do you call it?"

"Cupcake," he said abruptly.

"That's it? Don't you have to tell people what to expect?"

"I list the flavors. Coffee. Hazelnut. Vanilla. Nutmeg," he muttered.

"Oh, I see, you're like one of those trendy restaurants but they just list the ingredients." She grinned at him. "I really didn't have you down as a hipster."

He gave her an insulted look.

"I'm not. And I am not remotely trendy."

She ignored his protest and clapped her hands delightedly.

"I have a coffee with those same flavors. I have a great idea. You could call it a Speckled Owl cupcake, and I could give away coupons for one to anyone who ordered one of my Speckled Owl coffees."

"No," he said firmly, grateful that his grandmother wasn't there. He had no doubt she would also have thought it was a marvelous idea.

"Oh."

Her face fell, and he immediately wanted to retract his words and agree to her crazy scheme. Before he could make that mistake, she shrugged and smiled at him again.

"Never mind, that's not why I'm here. I brought you these."

She pulled her hand out from behind her back with the air of a magician. Six of the ugliest cupcakes he had ever seen were arranged on a pretty floral plate. They had been dusted with confectioners' sugar in an attempt to make them more appealing, but nothing could conceal the fact that they were lumpy, uneven, and at least two of them were suspiciously black.

"What are those?"

"Cupcakes, silly. I brought them as a peace offering. I'm really sorry we got off to such a bad beginning. They're for you."

Her big blue eyes were so hopeful that he couldn't help himself —he took the plate and as he did, their fingers touched, a spark of excitement immediately coursing through his body. From the way her breath caught, he suspected she felt it too.

"That was... nice of you," he said gruffly.

In a vain attempt to conceal his raging erection, he turned away to put the plate on his work counter, then picked up one of the cupcakes. One side was hard as a rock and the other suspiciously gooey, but she was watching him eagerly so he took a big bite—and immediately regretted it. He rushed over to the sink to spit it out, rinsing his mouth over and over to try and remove the disgusting taste.

"What the hell was that? Are you trying to poison me?" he growled, advancing on her.

She gave him a dismayed look, backing towards the door, and ended up pressed against it, looking up at him with wide eyes. He couldn't help remembering the last time they'd been in this position, and the resulting rush of desire only made him angrier.

"Is... is something wrong?"

"Did you taste the cupcakes, Elara?" he asked, his voice dangerously low.

"Well, no. I just made them for you. Is there something wrong with them?"

"That was the worst thing I have ever put in my mouth, and that includes the time that Eric tried to make me eat swamp mud. I was eight, and he's a troll. They mature early," he added as her eyes widened even more. "But at least that just tasted like mud. These taste like some kind of witch's potion—"

A terrible thought suddenly occurred to him. She had been spending a lot of time with Gladys Cravets—could she actually be trying to put some type of spell on him? Was that why even now he wanted to pull her into his arms and kiss her trembling lips until she smiled again?

"Did you try to put a spell on me?"

"A spell? What are you talking about?" Her apologetic look vanished as her small brows drew together in an adorable frown. "Why on earth would I want to put a spell on you?"

The tips of his ears began to burn, but he couldn't answer her.

Her eyes narrowed, and she stepped towards him, poking her finger at his chest. She winced, but didn't stop glaring.

"Believe me, I have no desire to put a spell on any one, especially not a too big, too grumpy, too annoying orc who manhandled my car for absolutely no reason!"

Each "too" was punctuated by another poke at his chest, and by the time she finished she was yelling.

Embarrassed, frustrated, and more than a little turned on, he did the only thing he could think of and snatched her up in his arms and kissed her. For one brief, glorious moment she kissed him back, but then she shuddered and pulled away, her expression horrified.

"Is that what those cupcakes taste like?"

The question shocked him back to reality, and he immediately put her back on the ground and retreated behind his counter, determined to put some distance between them.

She shuddered again. "I can see why you might think I was trying to poison you. But I wasn't."

He crossed his arms over his chest and glared at her.

"In that case, you should leave baking to the professionals. And coffee making."

Once again, her expression turned from apologetic to annoyed.

"I may not be able to bake, but I'm a damn good barista. You're just too pigheaded to admit it."

She stomped over to the door, delectable ass swaying, and slammed it behind her.

Fuck. He had to fight back the urge to go after her and tell her he hadn't meant it. Instead, he went into his store room and found the sandwich board he used to display occasional specials. He wrote "Real Coffee for Real Males" on it in large letters, then marched through the bakery and placed it next to his door where anyone entering Java Joy would be sure to see it. He gave a satisfied nod and returned to work.

His satisfaction lasted until his grandmother saw the sign, lectured him about it being discriminatory and unfriendly, and made him remove it. But he refused to surrender. There had to be some way to relieve himself of this troublesome female before he did something crazy—like carrying her back to his house, fucking her senseless, and keeping her forever.

CHAPTER 7

S now.

Elara looked out the window and smiled. Gladys and her coven had done an amazing job. The snow had started falling three days before today's Winter Festival. It had stopped late last night, and now everything was covered in a pretty blanket of white. Fairhaven Falls looked like a perfect winter postcard.

Even though it was still early, people were already heading for the town square. A tall blonde in a blue dress floated by below. She looked up at Elara and waved, sending a flurry of crystals towards her window, and she recognized Selene, the frost fairy who had helped the coven with their spell. Elara was used to seeing her in jeans and braids—she looked very different in the elegant gown with her hair down.

Inspired, she searched through her own wardrobe and chose a long cream sweater dress. It clung nicely to her curves before flaring out at the wrists and hem. Her fuzzy cream coat matched perfectly, and she added dangling crystal earrings and a delicate crystal necklace before setting off.

The town square was bustling with townspeople setting up their stalls and even a few early visitors. The food vendors were arranged around the outside of the square in matching candy-striped tents. She'd stocked hers last night and decorated it with strings of white lights. She had just started the coffee brewing when a big shadow marched by her tent.

Grondar. He'd been doing his best to avoid her since the cupcake incident, and she hadn't made any more attempts to soften him up. It hadn't stopped her from thinking—and dreaming—about him. His hair was down for once, although he'd pulled it back in a loose braid. His muscles strained against a plain, dark sweater that must be his version of dressing up, but he was wearing those faded jeans that hugged his amazing ass.

A little pulse of arousal went through her as she watched him scowling at his stall. His grandmother had insisted on placing it right next to hers, but apparently he hadn't realized it until now. After a disgusted glance at her pretty Java Joy sign, outlined in colored lights, he grabbed the sides of his tent and lifted. *Wow.* His muscles bulged beneath the sweater, but the weight didn't seem to bother him at all. He actually had the tent three feet up in the air when his grandmother came hurrying over. Today she was wearing a white bedazzled sweat-suit, and her eyes glittered like the sparkles on her suit as she glared at him.

"What the hell do you think you're doing?"

"Moving the tent," he grunted, easily holding the tent in midair.

"No, you're not. You put it down right now."

"But, Gran..."

"Now."

Flora looked like a miniature poodle confronting a mastiff, but Elara wasn't the least bit surprised when Grondar sighed and obeyed.

"Why did you put me next to *her*?" he demanded.

Ouch. Despite his grouchiness, she hadn't thought he disliked her that much. The words stung and her mouth threatened to tremble. A flash of what might have been remorse crossed his face, but it was gone so quickly it was difficult to know for sure.

"This is so cool."

A college-aged girl with a skinny boyfriend in tow distracted her. The girl was looking around eagerly, but her boyfriend looked less enthusiastic. Considering that the vast majority of Other males in the vicinity were about twice his size, she couldn't blame him.

"Do you have espresso?" the girl asked. "We left so early that I only had *one* cup of coffee this morning."

Her expression was so dramatic that Elara laughed.

"I sure do. I'm prepared for any caffeine emergency. Single or double?"

"Quad, please."

As Elara turned to the portable espresso machine she'd brought with her, the boyfriend scanned the board.

"What's in a Snow Bear?" he asked as the girl dreamily studied a big bear shifter.

"Coffee, white chocolate, and bravery," she said, ignoring the skeptical grunt from the stall next to hers.

"I'll have one of those."

By the time she'd finished making his drink, more people were starting to line up and she had no more time to worry about Grondar.

The festival was a huge success. Business remained steady all day, not just for her but for all the stalls she could see. Grondar even had to send for additional goods—apparently his food was delicious enough that most of the visitors were prepared to ignore his scowl.

The activities continued for several hours after the early winter sunset, and by the time it finally wound down, she was exhausted. Her feet hurt, her back ached, and her cheeks were stiff from smiling, but she still hummed happily as she started packing up her few remaining supplies.

"Closing so soon?"

The voice was low and seductive, the complete opposite of Grondar's usual growl, and she looked up to see a stranger smiling at her. A very handsome stranger with long dark hair, flamboyantly dressed in a flowing white linen shirt, a dark long-tailed coat, and dark pants tucked into knee-high boots. The outfit would have looked ridiculous on anyone else, but he wore it with a casual elegance that seemed completely natural.

"Did you want a coffee? I could probably still make you something," she said doubtfully.

"Do not concern yourself—I prefer other ways of quenching my thirst. I just wanted to make your acquaintance. I am Damian."

He smiled, revealing some extremely pointy teeth, and swept her a graceful bow.

"I'm pleased to meet you, Damian. I'm Elara."

"I know. Word of your beauty and intelligence has spread through our little town like wildfire."

He bowed again, pressing a slow, sensuous kiss to the back of her hand, his mouth cool and soft against her skin. He was precisely the type of man she'd always been attracted to—good-looking, charming, lean rather than bulky—but she didn't feel the slightest spark of interest. Certainly nothing like the tingle of excitement she experienced every time she and Grondar touched. But Grondar wasn't interested and Damian appeared to be, so she smiled at him.

"*Our* little town? Are you a native of Fairhaven Falls?"

"Not exactly, but I have lived here for many, many years. I know all the most delightful places. I was wondering if perhaps you would care to accompany me on a little tour?"

"No, she would not," a deep voice growled.

Grondar inserted himself between her and Damian, glowering at the other male.

"I don't believe I was asking you, Grondar."

Damian sounded amused rather than threatened even though Grondar towered over him.

"What the fuck are you playing at, Damian? You know vampires aren't allowed to seduce full humans."

Vampire? Oh. The elegant appearance, smooth manners, and sharp teeth suddenly made sense.

"Seducing? Merely by inviting a very attractive female to accompany me on a tour? I don't believe you understand seduction. But then you are out of practice, aren't you?"

Grondar growled again, taking a step towards the other male and she quickly put her hand on his arm.

"I'm sure Damian didn't mean any harm, but I'm afraid I already have plans for the evening."

"A pity. Perhaps another time."

The vampire swept another elegant bow and departed, if not exactly in a cloud of mist then with startling speed.

"Thank you," she said, smiling up at Grondar. "I didn't realize what he was."

His scowl didn't lessen.

"Of course you didn't. You can't be trusted on your own for a minute." His eyes swept over her body. "Or were you looking to be hunted?"

"What does that mean?"

"It means that if you dress up like bait, you have to expect someone to fall for the trap."

"Bait? Are you fricking kidding me? I'm just wearing a dress. And an apron!"

She'd abandoned her coat because she'd been so busy, but she'd tied a cute white apron over her dress.

His eyes swept over her again, lingering where the bib of the apron covered her breasts.

"It's not like any apron I've ever seen. It's designed to give a male... ideas."

His voice sounded hoarse, and then he traced a finger lightly along the lace ruffle on the upper swell of her breasts. All he touched was the soft knit of her dress, and it was the lightest possible touch, but desire streaked through her like lightning. Her nipples tingled, peaking beneath the fabric, and he groaned.

"Oh, fuck."

Then she was back in his arms and he was kissing her. There was no wall this time, but it didn't matter. He held her easily, one big arm beneath her butt and his other hand holding her head in place for his kiss. She didn't hesitate—her arms went around his neck as she kissed him back just as hard. He groaned into her mouth, and then his hand came down to cover her breast, closing around her with the perfect amount of pressure. His thumb swept back and forth across the taut peak and now it was her turn to groan, encouraging him to keep going.

He slid her down his body a little, enough for her to feel the tip of his shockingly large erection between her legs. *Oh my God.* She should have been intimidated. Instead, her clit throbbed with excitement. She tried to slide lower, to experience more of that tantalizing thickness. His hand went to her ass to help her and—"I'm glad to see you've made peace," Flora cackled.

Grondar put her down so fast that he almost dropped her. His hands lingered just long enough to make sure she was steady before he turned to glare at his grandmother.

"This is all your fault!"

"My fault? How is it my fault?"

Flora looked and sounded so saintly that Elara frowned at her. The old woman didn't have anything to do with the attraction between them. Did she?

"I don't know how it's your fault," Grondar roared. "But I know it is."

His eyes turned to her for the briefest second, then he stomped off.

"Excellent," Flora said.

She was actually rubbing her hands together gleefully like a comic book villain, and Elara frowned at her.

"What did he mean by that? Are you—or Gladys—doing something to make me feel this way?"

"What way is that, dear?"

Dark eyes twinkled at her, and she blushed. The last thing she wanted to do was discuss the way her body was still humming with arousal—and especially not with the grandmother of the male who'd caused it.

"Nothing," she muttered.

"All right then. The rest of the Council would like to have a little conversation about how today went."

"Right now?"

"Yes, so we can get everyone's first impressions. Unless you have other plans?"

Not since Grondar had chased off her first offer and then left her hanging.

"No, I'm free."

"Good. Then you can come with me. I'll arrange for everything in your stall to be returned to your shop in the meantime."

As she followed Flora, she couldn't help one last wistful glance in the direction in which Grondar had disappeared. But maybe it was just as well they'd been interrupted. She suspected that falling for him would only lead to heartbreak.

CHAPTER 8

*F*uck!

Grondar slammed his hand down on his work table hard enough to dent the metal. At least the bakery was already closed and no one appeared to ask him what was wrong. He certainly couldn't explain that in the four days since the Winter Festival he hadn't been able to get Elara out of his mind.

He'd thought about her often enough before, but after the Winter Festival it felt as if she were imprinted in his brain. The day had gone downhill from the moment he'd made that foolish remark and hurt her feelings. He'd wanted to retract it as soon as he spoke, but it was too late.

He'd spent the rest of the day trying to ignore the fact that she was only a few feet away, but it had been impossible. Every time he heard her infectious laugh, he wanted to look over and demand to know what was so funny. He was jealous of every happy smile she bestowed on her customers, wanting her to look at him that same way.

The dress she was wearing didn't help, lovingly outlining all those luscious curves. Every time she bent over the cooler at the back of the tent to reach for something, he wanted to step up behind her and hold her like that. As the day wore on and she had to reach further and further down, he snarled at any male who looked too long in her direction. Most of them were smart enough to look away, but of course Damian was the exception. The two of them were actually friends of a sort, but there was also a rivalry between them that dated back to their middle school years. As soon as Damian realized he was interested, he couldn't help provoking Grondar.

The fact that she didn't show any sign of being interested in the vampire gave him an enormous amount of satisfaction, but not enough to overcome his annoyance that he cared so much in the first place. But then they argued and she just looked so fucking adorable with her cheeks flushed and her eyes sparkling, that ridiculously provocative apron stretched across her chest, and he hadn't been able to resist kissing her.

He had the uneasy suspicion that if his grandmother hadn't shown up, he'd have had her skirt up and her body bent over the cooler just as he had been imagining all day. That knowledge and the lingering suspicion that his grandmother was somehow behind his unwanted attraction had only made him angrier.

He'd been doing his best to ignore Elara ever since, only moving between his home and the bakery, and by the grace of the gods had somehow managed to avoid seeing her. It hadn't helped. He still kept imagining he saw her face or caught her sweet scent or heard her soft voice.

"Grondar."

There it was again—her voice calling his name. It took him far longer than it should have to realize that she actually was calling him. He told himself to ignore her, but he stomped over to the kitchen door anyway and saw her crumpled on the ground at the bottom of their shared steps. Her face was white, tears pooling in those big, blue eyes as she looked up at him.

"I... I can't get up."

He was kneeling next to her before she finished speaking, lifting her off the ground and into his arms. She shuddered and clutched at his shirt.

"What the hell happened?" he asked, his voice rough with anxiety.

"I think there must have been some ice on the last step. My foot just went out from under me."

Fuck! Either because of the witches' spell or because the temperatures had finally caught up with the season, the weather had been icy and damp ever since the festival. He tried to keep the steps and pathway salted, but he must have missed a spot. His voice turned even gruffer as he looked down at the sexy little heeled boots she was wearing, sexy boots that had starred in his dreams but were completely inappropriate for the weather.

"You have to learn to be more careful," he began. "Try thinking before—"

To his horror, she burst into tears. *Double fuck.* He immediately stopped lecturing her and hugged her to his chest, rocking her back and forth like a child. She sobbed into his shirt for a few more minutes before sniffing dejectedly and giving him a watery smile.

"I'm sorry. I should have been more careful."

"It's not your fault," he found himself telling her, anxious to replace that woebegone expression. "I've been salting the steps, so you probably didn't realize that they were icy."

She gave him another tremulous smile.

"We can argue about whose fault it is once I feel better. Could you... could you help me upstairs to my apartment?"

"Of course," he said roughly, annoyed at himself for not having thought about getting her out of the cold.

He rose to his feet, still holding her cradled against his chest, and carried her to her back door—her unlocked back door. Fighting back the urge to lecture her again about her disregard for her own safety, he stomped up the stairs to her apartment.

The living room had sheets tacked up over the windows and no furniture except for one lone chair. Stacks of boxes apparently served as footrest and side table. It was completely unsuitable for her at the best of times and especially in her current condition. He carried her through the kitchenette and past a small bathroom to the back bedroom. Once again, it had sheets tacked over the windows and minimal furniture—an air mattress and a stack of boxes holding a lamp. More boxes were stacked against the far wall, obviously filled with clothing, including one that contained a tantalizing mixture of silks and lace in a variety of colors.

He actually turned around twice as if he expected additional furniture to suddenly appear.

"This is where you're living?"

"Well, yes."

She didn't meet his gaze, studying her small fingers instead as they toyed with one of the buttons on his shirt.

"I gave away all my old furniture, and I only ordered a few new things. I wanted to get a feel for the place before I added too much. Unfortunately, I've been so busy that I haven't had a chance to look for anything. The furniture I did order was delayed, and now it's been stuck in Charlotte since it started snowing."

He took another look at the air mattress, realizing that in addition to not providing enough support, it was so low to the ground that it would be impossible for her to get in and out of it with an injured ankle. She couldn't stay here.

He sighed, turned around once more, and stomped back down the stairs.

"Where... where are you taking me?" she asked, her voice unsteady.

"Somewhere more suitable." He stopped as he reached the kitchen door. "Keys."

She bit her lip, then dug into the pocket of her extremely tight jeans to pull them out and silently hand them to him. Sternly ignoring how good it felt to have her wiggling against him like that, he stepped through the door, locked it behind them, and marched back to his truck. He carefully placed her sideways on the bench seat in the back of the cab so that her legs would remain elevated, then fastened the seat belt around her. Her face was even paler now, but she did her best to smile at him, and he ran a finger down the silky softness of her cheek.

"Don't worry, sugar. Everything's going to be all right."

The words were out before he could call them back, and he was immediately appalled. He quickly slammed the door shut and climbed into the driver's seat. To his relief, she didn't say anything, although when he snuck a glance at her in the rearview mirror, he could see her watching him thoughtfully.

He told himself that he was taking her to his grandmother, but when the time came, he passed the turnoff to her street and went around the block to his house. *It's only because my main bedroom and bath are downstairs*, he told himself, but couldn't ignore the immense feeling of satisfaction that filled him when he carried her over the threshold and had her in his house at last.

"Your door wasn't locked," she immediately pointed out.

"That's because I'm not a pretty, helpless little human. Nobody in town is dumb enough to mess with me."

"Pretty?" she whispered, her smile flashing for an instant before she frowned, her small brows drawing together. Why the fuck did she look so adorable when she did that?

"I'm not helpless," she insisted, making an even more adorable attempt to look fierce.

"If I put you on your feet, could you stand?"

"Well, no, that's because I injured—"

"Helpless," he said firmly and carried her through into his bedroom.

No doubt he could have come up with a number of reasons why it was a better choice than the guest room, but none of those occurred to him at the time. All he wanted was to see her in his bed. Another surge of satisfaction filled him as he placed her gently against the pillows. She looked as perfect there as he had envisioned—although in his imagination she was usually wearing much less clothing.

Her eyes widened again as she looked around.

"What a gorgeous bed. Whose room is this?"

A wood elf had created the bed from discarded branches, stripping the bark and polishing the wood until it glowed. Each of the four posts rose like a separate tree, but their branches wove together over the bed to form an intricate canopy intertwined with tiny sparkling lights. He'd wanted it since the first moment he saw it, but it looked even more perfect holding her. She reached over and stroked the polished wood of one of the posts and his cock jerked with frustrated jealousy. He wanted her hands on him, not on his bed.

"It's mine." The tips of his ears were burning again.

"Thank you for bringing me here," she said, smiling up at him.

She reached out her hand towards him, but he was afraid if he touched her now while she was in his bed, his house, he wouldn't be able to stop himself from mating her. He ignored her outstretched hand, his aching cock, and the pain in his chest.

"I'll arrange for a doctor," he said gruffly, and hurried out of the room.

CHAPTER 9

*E*lara stared after Grondar and sighed. He was the most confusing male she'd ever met. In addition to his grumpy facade and searing kisses, she kept getting tantalizing hints that there was so much more to him. She'd never been as glad to see anyone in her life as she had been when the door opened and he came stomping down the stairs towards her. She didn't even care that he was lecturing her as long as he was holding her close against his huge, warm body. And then he'd brought her to his house. Considering his usual attitude, she'd frequently imagined him living in a cave, beating his chest towards outsiders. She certainly hadn't expected this cozy little cottage.

Cozy, yes, but not at all little, she amended, looking around. The arched multi-paned windows, built-in bookcases, and wood framed fireplace were definitely cozy, but the scale was not. The fireplace mantel would be over her head, and the bed itself could have held two people of Grondar's size.

He probably wanted it this large because he had some statuesque orc girlfriend, she thought, then scowled. Would he kiss her the way he did if he had a girlfriend?

She'd certainly never seen him with an orc female—or any other female for that matter. Flora had told her once that he preferred his solitude, and she had no difficulty believing it. As attractive as it was, the cottage could certainly benefit from a woman's touch. Perhaps some brightly patterned cushions on the window seats beneath the arched windows, or a soft throw on the big chair in front of the fireplace.

She was busily deciding on decorative touches to improve the place when she heard the front door open. Her heart skipped a beat. He'd said no one would mess with his house, but what if he was wrong? She breathed a sigh of relief when Flora poked her head around the door and grinned at her.

"There you are. I was hoping he was smart enough to bring you here."

"You knew?"

"About ten seconds after he roared off down the alley with you in his truck. This is a small town—and you know Gladys would never keep me in the dark."

"I suppose not. Why did you think he would bring me here?"

Elara hummed noncommittally as she bent over to examine Elara's ankle.

"That looks nasty. I'll tell Gladys we do need her after all."

"Need her? For what?"

"To heal your ankle, of course. She heard you cry out and was on her way over when my grandson decided to swoop to the rescue." Flora's eyes twinkled. "But now that he's been all heroic and rescued you, we females will do the real work and fix you up."

"He said he was going to get a doctor," she protested.

Flora rolled her eyes. "I expect he's gone to fetch Jeremiah. He's not a doctor, he's a witch doctor—"

"Which is a completely inappropriate title," Gladys snapped as she marched in followed by two other members of her coven. "He has absolutely nothing to do with us or we with him."

The older woman's cheeks were flushed, and Elara gave her a curious glance. Why did she suspect that there was something more than professional jealousy at work? Gladys sniffed and bent over her ankle.

"Now then. Let's take a look at this ankle."

She ran her fingers very gently over the swollen ankle, but Elara winced anyway.

"Don't you worry, dearie. I'll get that fixed right up." She turned to one of her acolytes. "Did you bring the healing potion?"

"Yes, mistress." The woman handed over an ancient leather satchel with trembling hands. "And I added the herbs you requested."

"That's a good girl. Now go stand over there until I need you."

Both women immediately backed up against the far wall. For all the witch's friendliness, she was in complete control of her coven and, Elara suspected, had a good deal of power.

Gladys poured a small amount of bright red liquid into a wooden cup and started to raise it to Elara's lips.

"What is that?"

"I told you—it's a healing potion."

"What's in it?" she asked suspiciously.

"Eye of newt. Toe of frog. That kind of thing," Gladys said eerily, then laughed. "You should see your face. I assure you it's nothing harmful, although I'm not about to reveal the actual ingredients to anyone outside the coven. Now drink."

There was enough command in the witch's voice that she obeyed. To her relief, it was very tasty, berry-like with a slight bitter aftertaste. She found herself licking the bowl of the cup to get the last drops.

"Good. Now you just lie back against the pillows while we work."

Once again, she obeyed and as she did, the surge of warmth ran through her veins. Mmm. This was extremely pleasant. She didn't feel as if she were drunk exactly, but everything seemed to be wrapped in a warm, rosy glow. She winced again as Gladys lowered the zipper on her boot, but the witch murmured a few unintelligible words and the pain vanished. Her ankle was bathed in some cool substance, then wrapped tightly in a bandage, various herbs tucked between each layer. Gladys tied an extravagant bow, then sat back and smiled at her.

"There. The bandage will stay in place until I remove it. Just stay off your ankle for another twenty-four hours and you'll be as good as new."

It took a moment for the words to penetrate her rosy haze.

"Twenty-four hours? I can't shut down the coffee shop for that long—"

"You won't have to," a voice growled, and then Grondar appeared. "Ermengarde recommended someone to help you out, and I've already made the arrangements."

"Who?"

"Annie Carlyle."

The name meant nothing to her, but Flora nodded approvingly.

"The brownie? An excellent idea. I don't know why I didn't think of it myself."

"Because you were too busy interfering in my life. What are all these people doing in my bedroom? I told Elara that I was going to get a doctor," he said through gritted teeth and stepped aside to reveal another male.

The newcomer had deep brown skin and short iron gray curls. He was neatly dressed in a dark three-piece suit, and he could have been any businessman in the city except for the big, colorful necklace he was wearing that combined dried herbs, strips of leather, beads, and crystals, and—were those tiny skulls?

The newcomer paid no attention to her, his eyes fixed on the woman at her bedside.

"Hello, Gladys. It's been a long time," he said quietly. For a moment, the witch's face softened, but then her shoulders snapped back and she glared at him.

"Not long enough, Jeremiah."

The man sighed and turned to Grondar.

"If Gladys has already healed her, there is nothing for me to do here."

"Don't you want to check her work?" he growled, shooting a suspicious glance at the four women now gathered around the bed.

Jeremiah shook his head.

"There is no need. Gladys is an excellent healer."

He gave Gladys an old-fashioned bow, then walked out of the room. Elara saw Gladys's mouth open, but she snapped it shut without saying anything.

"Fine. Thank you," Grondar snapped. "Now all of you get the hell out of my house."

Flora marched up to him and twisted the skin of his arm just above his elbow. To Elara's shock, he winced.

"Mind your manners, boy. I taught you better than that."

He visibly took a deep breath, then nodded.

"Thank you for coming to Elara's aid in healing her ankle. I am sure she appreciates it."

Although he had modulated his voice, he was obviously still speaking through gritted teeth and Flora shook her head.

"I suppose under the circumstances I'll accept that. Come on, girls. We'll leave Grondar to look after Elara." Flora gave her a warm smile. "We'll check on you again tomorrow, dear."

Flora, Gladys, and the other two women walked past him as if he didn't exist. He gave a satisfied nod, then a sudden look of panic crossed his face.

"What do they mean, look after you?"

He darted after them, but Elara had heard the click of the front door closing and knew he was too late. She settled back against the pillows and smiled, the warm glow from the healing potion still lingering in her veins as Grondar stomped back into the room. His dark eyes heated as he looked at her, and she deliberately stretched, knowing the movement would bring her breasts into even greater prominence. He took a half-step towards her, and she held her breath in anticipation. She knew she might get hurt, but playing with fire had never been so satisfying. To her disappointment, he didn't come any closer.

She couldn't resist dropping her gaze, her breath catching at the massive erection clearly visible beneath the weathered jeans.

"What do you need?" he asked begrudgingly.

"Right now, I'd love some supper. I've been too busy to eat anything all day. Then later I'll need your help taking my clothes off, and I'd love a bath."

She was quite sure the cottage had a magnificent bathroom.

He made a strangled noise, and she watched in fascination as his cock seemed to grow another impossible inch.

"I'll make you something to eat," he growled and strode away.

She half-expected him not to return, but in a surprisingly short time he returned with a tray—a white bed tray carved with delicate vines—that he placed carefully over her legs.

"It was a gift from Gran," he said, obviously interpreting her astonished expression as he lifted the covers off the dishes. "Soup. Tomato. Scones. Also tomato, with a slice of local cheddar."

"Hipster," she murmured teasingly.

The food was unadorned and presented on sturdy white china, but it smelled delicious. She took a big spoonful of the soup, then moaned appreciatively. The soup contained a combination of roasted and fresh tomatoes, the two preparations complementing each other, with a variety of subtle seasonings and a fine chiffonade of basil.

"This is so good. You should really call it something more appealing."

"You'd probably call it something like Tomato Joy," he said absently, and she realized she was staring at her mouth.

She licked her lips and smiled at him.

"Probably. Or maybe Childhood Remembered."

He frowned, looking up from her mouth to her eyes.

"That's not how I remember my childhood."

"Your parents never made you tomato soup? Or Flora?" she added, remembering that his parents died when he was young.

He shrugged. "If my parents did, I don't remember it. I doubt they had time—we were always on the road to somewhere. And Gran likes to bake but she doesn't like regular cooking. We ate a lot of sandwiches."

She laughed and picked up one of the scones, perfectly buttered and toasted, the cheese just slightly melted.

"If the sandwiches were like this, I wouldn't object."

"They weren't." When she didn't respond, he added with obvious reluctance, "Back then the bakery only served sweets."

"The bakery? It's your Gran's bakery?"

"It was," he said. "I bought it from her."

Clearly uncomfortable, he changed the subject. "Did your parents make you tomato soup?"

"Yes. And before you ask, I had a perfectly normal childhood with perfectly normal, perfectly nice parents who have absolutely no idea why I decided to move here."

"Why did you?"

She sighed. "Last year was a horrible year. I walked in on my former fiancé with someone else. I broke up with him, and then he fired me. He was my boss, and yes, I know it was stupid to get involved with him in the first place. Somehow he made it seem like it was perfectly normal. He was very... charming."

"I am not charming."

"No—thank goodness." She grinned at him. "Anyway, I was looking for a new job and I had several offers, but the more I thought about spending the rest of my life in the corporate world, the more I disliked the idea. I'd spent a long time trying to be as perfectly normal and perfectly nice as my parents, and I was tired of it. I decided to make a new life for myself. I stumbled on the advertisement for the storefront, and as soon as I saw the pictures of Fairhaven Falls, I knew this was where I wanted to be."

"Do you still feel that way?"

His voice deepened as he leaned closer, his face only a short distance away from hers.

"I'm absolutely sure."

She expected him to kiss her, but instead he jumped up and picked up the tray.

"I'm going to wash the dishes."

She recognized the retreat, but retained enough of the rose-colored confidence from the healing potion to call after him.

"Just hurry back. I still need you to help me take a bath."

He dropped the tray.

CHAPTER 10

*D*amn *female,* Grondar grumbled to himself as he cleaned up the mess from the tray he'd dropped. Fortunately the sturdy china hadn't broken and neither had Gran's tray. Even though he'd thought it a ridiculous present, he appreciated the artistry of the design—even more now that he'd used it to serve *his* female *his* food in *his* bed.

Fuck. Not his female. But his denial couldn't completely eliminate his pleasure at feeding her—at caring for her. And now she wanted him to bathe her? He had imagined her flushed and glowing in a tub once before, but the thought of her in his tub was even more pleasurable. What was he going to do? He cleaned up as slowly as possible before finally returning to his bedroom, as nervous as he had once been on the first day of school.

She looked up when he finally returned to the bedroom and smiled as if she were delighted to see him. His chest suddenly ached, and he frowned at her.

"I'll call Gran and ask her to help you," he said quickly.

"I'm sure she would have been happy to help me—before you threw her out of your house."

He had an uneasy suspicion she was right. It would be just like his grandmother to ignore his calls, and no doubt Gladys would behave the same way.

"I could call Ermengarde," he offered almost desperately.

"The pixie with the pink hair? She seems very nice, but I don't know anything about her other than that she likes Speckled Owls."

"You don't know me either," he burst out.

Her teasing expression softened.

"Yes, I do, Grondar. And I trust you."

Fuck. How could he resist, especially when she seemed so sincere. *Human females are never sincere*, he reminded himself as he stomped off to the bathroom to run water into the tub, but the familiar caution rang hollow. Despite his initial accusation that she was trying to sabotage him, everything about her seemed genuine. He sighed, then threw a couple of vanilla beans into the tub, letting the familiar scent perfume the air as he lit the row of candles on the ledge above the tub.

After making sure the water wasn't too hot, he returned to carry her into the bathroom. He lifted her into his arms, trying to ignore the fact that she felt just as right in his arms now as she had when he brought her home. As he carried her into the bathroom, she gave a delighted gasp.

"I knew you had a wonderful bathroom. This is gorgeous."

He couldn't help smiling at her approval. The same wood elf who had built his bed had also carved the posts that framed all the bathroom fixtures. The tub was set in a bay window with more carved trees forming an arched opening in front of it. The soft shades of blue and green in the stained-glass window sparkled in the candlelight.

"And candles too?" Her body suddenly stiffened. "Do you have a girlfriend, Grondar?"

"No," he said gruffly, his own body tensing. "This is just how I like to relax."

"I'm sorry, I didn't mean—"

"Hold on to the counter," he ordered, bending her over his arm so he could remove her pants without putting her on her feet, and she obeyed silently.

He hoped the reminder of the reason for his solitary status would soften his rampaging lust. It didn't. His cock pressed painfully against his pants as he wrestled her tight jeans down over that lush, perfect ass, leaving her in nothing but tiny baby blue underwear. He wanted desperately to curve his hands over all that glowing flesh, but he couldn't. He was afraid that if he did, he'd end up carrying her back to his bed and claiming her.

"What about my panties?" she asked breathlessly.

When he didn't respond, she had the nerve to actually wiggle that tempting ass at him. He smacked her, just hard enough to sting, and the sugary scent of her arousal increased.

"Wash around them." His voice was a hoarse growl as he smoothed his hand over the pretty pink flesh, then tugged at the back strap of her underwear, tightening it against her sex. "There's not enough of them to get in the way."

She ignored his words, pushing back against him and he smacked the other cheek.

"Stop that," he repeated, even as he stroked the heated flesh.

"Grondar, please."

His control broke. He pulled her back against him, her lush ass cushioning his cock for one glorious moment. But he had forgotten about her ankle, and when he fumbled between them to free his erection, he accidentally brushed against her ankle and she cried out. *Fuck!* Forcing his arousal back under control, he carefully lifted her higher, then turned her so that she was sitting on the counter instead.

"Raise your hands," he ordered, his voice almost unrecognizable.

Her eyes had deepened to midnight blue, but she obeyed silently, lifting her arms over her head. He carefully removed her thick sweater, doing his best to ignore the feeling of her silky soft skin against his fingers as he pulled it up over her head. He knew he shouldn't look, but he did anyway.

Her bountiful breasts were barely contained by a lacy blue bra that matched her underwear. The lace was so sheer that he could see the deep pink of the areolae surrounding her luscious nipples. Mesmerized, he ran a finger across one of those impudent peaks, just as he had once before, but this was even better with only the thin layer of lace between them. She took a quick breath, her breasts threatening to break free from the flimsy covering.

"You're so pretty, sugar."

"I'm glad you think so," she whispered, a tide of pink washing over her face. "I was thinking of you when I put these on."

His first reaction was pleasure, his hands tightening over her breasts, but then he had a sudden flashback. Gwendolyn had told him something similar once when he came home unexpectedly and found her in black lingerie. But she'd been lying. She'd been wearing it for her human boyfriend. He didn't want to believe that Elara was anything like Gwendolyn, but he'd been fooled before. His hands dropped to her waist, and he picked her up and carried her over to the bath, careful to keep her at arm's length. She gave him a puzzled frown.

"What are you doing?"

"You said you wanted a bath," he said grimly and lowered her carefully into the water.

Despite his care, he had forgotten one thing—the tub had been designed for him and she was considerably smaller. As soon as he released her, her head disappeared beneath the water.

Oh, shit. He quickly pulled her back to a sitting position as she coughed and spluttered. Water dripped down her face as she gave him that adorable glare, looking as outraged as a wet kitten. Despite his best attempt to maintain his composure, he started to laugh. She sputtered for a moment longer, then grinned ruefully.

"It's not my fault you're so damn big."

"I'm sorry, sugar. I should have realized. Here, hold on to this for just a second."

He put her hands on the side of the tub and made sure she was steady before stepping back.

"I can't wash like this."

"I know," he said, and started shedding his clothes.

CHAPTER 11

*O*h. My. God.

Whoever coined the expression "built like a god" had obviously never seen a naked orc. Elara clutched the edge of the tub as she stared at Grondar. The lower half of his body was as thickly muscled as his upper body with thick thighs and sturdy calves, but her gaze snagged on his cock. He was the same basic shape as a man, but she didn't believe any mere mortal had ever had such a long, thick cock. In addition to the sheer size, an elaborate ridged pattern covered his shaft, and the cherry on the top of the perfect cock sundae was the series of metal balls that laddered down the underside.

"You pierced your cock?"

"Obviously," he said shortly but despite the rough response, she could see his shaft flex as she studied him.

"And are those markings some kind of tattoo?"

"Yes."

"Didn't it hurt?"

"Yes. Now do you have any more questions, or can I get in the tub before you manage to drown yourself?"

"I have a lot more questions, but I don't want to drown."

He shook his head, but his mouth twisted into a smile. Damn, he looked good when he smiled—and even better when he laughed. Even though his amusement had been at her expense, she enjoyed seeing him so relaxed. Now she couldn't decide if he was hotter when he was frowning or when he was laughing. Or was he just hot no matter what?

She was still pondering the question when he climbed into the tub behind her and tugged her back into his arms. *No matter what,* she decided as she snuggled against that big, broad chest, feeling remarkably safe despite the massive cock flexing beneath her butt.

"If it hurt, why did you do it?"

He sighed. "It is an orc custom—the markings and the piercings are designed to enhance a female's pleasure."

"Oh." She pondered his question for a moment. "Did you do it for a specific female?"

The muscles in his arms and chest were so tense they almost vibrated.

"Yes, but it was a mistake."

"Why?"

"I do not wish to discuss it."

"Oh, come on. I told you all about my cheating bastard of an ex."

He didn't respond and she looked up to see him frowning into the distance. Despite the frown, there was an unexpected vulnerability in his eyes, and she gave his chest a gentle pat.

"Well, if she cheated on you, she was a complete idiot."

He looked down at her.

"Why do you say that?"

"Because all this..." she gestured at his body "...deserves to be appreciated."

His cock jerked again, hard enough that it actually lifted her a little. Holy crap.

He leaned down as if he were going to kiss her, then stopped, his nostrils flaring.

"Did Gladys give you a healing potion?"

"Yep." She licked her lips reminiscently. "It was delicious."

"No wonder," he sighed.

"No wonder what?"

"No wonder you're saying these things. The healing potion acts like an intoxicant."

"I do feel very relaxed," she admitted. "And everything has a pretty pink tinge to it. But—" She poked his chest, forgetting that it was like poking a wall. "But that doesn't mean I'm not telling you the truth. In vino veritas and all that."

He looked torn, then shook his head.

"I think we'd better confine our activities to bathing."

"Okay," she agreed and smiled up at him before settling back against his chest.

"You do not wish to wash yourself?"

"Since you seem to think I'm too intoxicated to know what I'm saying, I must be too intoxicated to bathe myself. You're going to have to do it."

His cock jerked so hard it threatened to throw her off his lap.

"Fuck," he muttered under his breath—but he reached for the soap.

Not surprisingly, he had plain white soap, but it glided smoothly over her skin and left it feeling silky soft. He started with her hands, even sliding his big fingers between hers to make sure he was doing a good job. He worked his way up her arms in long, soothing strokes. He washed her neck and the upper slope of her breasts above the edge of her bra, then hesitated. Her nipples were throbbing so hard they ached, but she managed to keep her voice light.

"Don't worry, they won't bite."

"But I might," he growled against her ear and she quivered.

Despite his initial hesitation, he proceeded to cover her breasts with a firm grip, massaging the soap into them through the thin lace. The sight of his huge green hands working her breasts was the most erotic thing she'd ever seen, and the texture of the lace against her skin only heightened her pleasure. She arched against him, silently asking for more.

"I warned you what would happen if you wiggled," he growled. "Do you want me to spank these pretty tits of yours?"

"You wouldn't! Would you?"

And why did the thought excite her?

"Not as long as you're a good girl."

She did her best to relax against him and he growled his approval. He clamped down on her nipples, tugging firmly, and a sudden, unexpected climax washed over her, leaving her trembling against him.

"Wow. That's never happened before."

Perhaps he was right about the healing potion. She hadn't intended to confess that.

"Perhaps no one has ever touched you properly before, sugar."

"Hmm." She smiled up at him over her shoulder. "Then I wonder what else you could do that no one's ever done properly before."

He hesitated, and she held her breath, but then his hands left her breasts and moved down over her stomach. He ran the soap over them in what she was sure was not intended to be a seductive manner, but she was already so sensitive that everything he did added to her arousal. He skipped over the area covered by her panties and proceeded to her legs, cupping a foot in one big hand and pulling it towards him. He washed her calf and her thigh, stopping just before she wanted him to, then repeated the process on the other leg before starting to put down the soap.

"I think you forgot something."

"I didn't forget anything," he growled, and she could feel his cock throbbing against her ass.

"You wouldn't want me to go to bed dirty, would you? Or do you want me to take off my panties and wash myself?"

She reached for the thin strip of lace across her hips, and he put his hand over hers.

"No. Those are going to stay on."

She suspected he knew as well as she did that the tiny lace panties weren't an actual barrier. He could easily sweep them to one side if he wanted to, but if it made him feel better that she was wearing them, she wouldn't object. Too much.

He curled his finger around the band and tugged, just as he had earlier, and just as it had before, the pressure pulled the lace tightly against her swollen clit. Hard enough to tantalize but not hard enough to achieve climax. She wanted to arch against him, but she remembered his warning. Would he spank her again if she did?

The thought of that delicious little sting was not exactly a deterrent. In fact, she wouldn't mind if he did do it again. He seemed to read her mind because he placed his other hand firmly over her hip to hold her in place.

"No wiggling," he warned. "Remember, bad girls get spanked."

"What do good girls get?"

"Pleasure," he growled and slid a finger down over that taut strip of lace.

The thick digit forced her lips apart, exposing her completely to that wonderful, tormenting touch. She grabbed his massive forearms in a vain attempt to remain still.

"Good girl," he growled in her ear, then pinched her clit.

If her first climax had been a wave of pleasure, this was a tsunami, sending her into a swirling maelstrom of pleasure that seemed to go on and on until it finally subsided, leaving her limp and trembling in his arms. As soon as she stopped trembling, he finished washing her, then lifted her out of the tub and sat her back on the counter while he dried her off.

He hesitated over her underwear, then disappeared for a moment, returning with one of his shirts. He dropped it over her head, then reached beneath it and undid her bra and slid down her panties. As much as she enjoyed the brush of his fingers against her skin, her arousal had been replaced by exhaustion, and she sat there quietly until he finished and carried her to the bed.

She was already half-asleep when he put her down, but she was awake enough to realize that he wasn't joining her. She cracked open one eye to find him standing over the bed watching her.

"Aren't you coming to bed too?"

"I..."

It was the first time she had ever seen him at a loss for words. If she hadn't been so sleepy, she would have been triumphant.

"You shouldn't leave the patient alone," she said, doing her best to give him a pitiful look.

He shook his head, but he dimmed the lights and a moment later he climbed in on the other side of the bed. He'd left a wide gap between them, but to hell with that. She wiggled her way across the bed and snuggled against the reassuring warmth of his side. That was better. The last thing she felt before she drifted off to sleep was his arm coming around to hold her.

CHAPTER 12

This is a bad idea.

Despite that conviction, Grondar couldn't force himself to release Elara. When was the last time he'd held a warm, sweet-smelling female in his arms? Even when he and Gwendolyn had been at what he thought was the most intense stage of their relationship, she'd never wanted him to spend the night. And she'd never felt as soft, as perfect in his arms as Elara did.

But even if she really were attracted to him, and it wasn't just the influence of the healing potion, it didn't mean she had any interest in a permanent relationship. And he didn't do casual. He'd had his share of offers from human females attracted by his size, but all they'd wanted was a quick fling with the big bad orc. He wasn't interested in that.

Even if he did decide to take a chance, what were the odds she would stick around? Based on what she'd told him, she'd had a good life in the city until the previous year. She'd changed her entire life to move to Fairhaven Falls—she could just as easily decide to return to her previous life. Despite the Council's best efforts, full humans didn't tend to last long in town.

Yet despite all the arguments battling it out in his head—and the persistent ache in his neglected cock—holding her in his arms filled him with something that felt oddly like contentment. He breathed in her sweet sugar scent and fell asleep.

He slept better than he had in ages—deeply and dreamlessly until erotic images started to dance through his head. Elara bent over the counter and smiling at him over her shoulder. Her creamy breasts framed by his big hands. On her knees in front of him, taking him into that pretty pink mouth as he gripped her ponytail. He could almost feel her small tongue circling the head of his cock and exploring his piercings. His hips jerked upwards, and he heard her gasp. His eyes flew open.

The room was still dark, but orcs were predators and his night vision was more than adequate enough to see her kneeling over him, her small hand trying to surround him, and a sparkle of mischief in her eyes. She was still wearing his shirt, but the neckline had slipped down enough to reveal the plump swell of her breasts.

"Before you say anything, the healing potion has completely worn off, there's no pink glow, and I am doing this strictly because I want to."

Before he could format a response, she leaned forward and licked the tip of his cock again. *Oh, fuck.*

"Elara," he groaned.

"Hush. For once in your life, just relax and enjoy."

She tugged very gently at one of his piercings with her teeth, and he shuddered.

"Did that hurt?" she asked anxiously.

"Fuck, no. Do it again, sugar."

She hummed happily and obeyed, working her way down the line of metal balls before grinning up at him.

"I guess the pain was worth it."

"That's not why I did it," he groaned. "They stimulate your clit from inside."

Her eyes widened, and the sweet scent of her arousal intensified. He gripped the mattress as hard as he could trying to prevent himself from flipping her over and demonstrating just how good they would feel inside her.

She hummed again, then ran her finger lightly over the raised lines of his ritual tattoo, her touch agonizingly gentle.

"And these?"

"More stimulation."

"How—"

"Sugar, I promise I will answer all your questions later, but now, for the love of all the gods, put your pretty mouth on me again."

To his eternal gratitude, she did, following the lines of his tattoo back up his shaft.

"Harder," he growled as she licked teasingly across the broad head of his cock.

This time, she scraped lightly with her teeth, and he buried his hand in her hair, urging her on. Her lips parted, and somehow she managed to take the entire head of his cock in her small mouth, surrounding him with tight, wet heat. She circled her tongue around his top piercing, sending a jolt of pleasure down his spine, but it wasn't until she looked up at him, eyes shining, that he exploded. Afraid of choking her, he managed to pull free, shuddering helplessly as long spurts of creamy seed splashed across her cheek and dripped down onto her chest, marking her.

More seed covered his own stomach, but he ignored it, watching intently as she licked her lips before smiling at him.

"Mmm. You didn't have to pull out."

He would have sworn she had drained him completely, but his cock jerked again at her words.

"Maybe I like seeing you covered in my seed."

He stroked his thumb across her cheek, massaging the creamy liquid into her skin, then stopped, horrified. What the fuck was he doing? Primitive orc males had marked their females this way, but he was not one of his savage ancestors—and she was not his female.

"I'll get a towel," he muttered and fled to the bathroom.

What the fuck am I doing? She is not mine.

He returned to the bedroom with a damp cloth and forced himself to remove his seed from her skin, hating each swipe of the cloth. She only gave him a sleepy smile.

When he was done, he pulled the blankets up around her and returned to the bathroom, waiting until he was sure she was asleep before emerging. He wanted more than anything to climb back into the bed and pull her into his arms, but he couldn't. He wouldn't. He'd thought Gwendolyn had hurt him —that would be nothing to the damage that Elara could cause if he allowed himself to get close to her and then she left him.

He walked out of the bedroom and went to seek comfort in his kitchen.

Elara wasn't entirely surprised when she woke up alone. For reasons she didn't really understand, he was clearly fighting the attraction between them. But as frustrating as she found it, it was also oddly reassuring that he wasn't trying to rush her into bed the way most of the men she dated usually did.

And he'd left her breakfast.

The tray was sitting on the nightstand, complete with a thermos of coffee. She poured a cup and took a cautious sip. To her surprise it was extremely good. Maybe she hadn't given his "real coffee" enough credit. An insulated lid covered a plate with a perfectly cooked omelet, accompanied by a sliced avocado. She sighed happily and dug in.

Just as she was finishing, Flora popped her head round the door.

"Good morning, dear."

Elara smiled at her. "You came back."

"The boy called and apologized very nicely before he asked me to come and stay with you. How are you feeling?"

"My ankle is still a little sore, but overall much better."

"Nothing like a peaceful night in a big orc bed to make you feel better." Flora's eyes twinkled. "That is, I assume it was peaceful?"

Nothing could prevent the tide of color rising in her cheeks, but she managed to nod.

"I wish I was surprised," Flora muttered.

"What do you mean?"

The older woman hesitated, then sat down on the bed next to her.

"Do you like my grandson?"

"You know I do," she said quietly. "But I'm not sure he likes me."

"Oh, he definitely likes you. But he was burned once, very badly, by a pretty human female. Pretty in the face, anyway," Flora sniffed. "Her insides were as ugly as they get."

"What happened?"

"Grondar decided very early that he wanted to be a baker and work in the bakery. I didn't push him, mind."

"I'm sure you didn't."

"He decided that he needed additional instruction so he applied to the culinary institute in the capital and of course they accepted him." Flora sighed. "He was only eighteen although he was almost as big as he is now. But he didn't have any real experience with females. Maybe that's why Gwendolyn was able to get her claws into him."

"What did she do?"

"Used him every way she could. He helped her cook, taught her recipes, let her take credit for his ideas. I could see what was happening, but I knew he wouldn't listen to me. As it got closer to graduation, they announced that the top chef in the class would be offered the chance for a very prestigious internship with a Michelin star restaurant."

"Let me guess," she said, her heart aching. "Gwendolyn got the offer."

"Yep. He sacrificed his own chance to help her, and as soon as it was announced, she dropped him like a hot potato and took off for California with the human boyfriend she'd been seeing the whole time."

"Poor Grondar. What did he do?"

"Came home and took over the bakery." Flora sighed. "I honestly don't think he minded losing the internship—he'd always wanted to be here—but her betrayal scarred him. He has trust issues," she added, and Elara couldn't help laughing.

"I did notice. It makes me so angry for him."

"I understand. I almost took off for California to teach her a lesson." Flora flashed her sharp teeth in a fierce smile. "But he needed me. And Gladys talked me out of having the coven put a spell on her. She said that kind of thing always backfires."

"I can understand why you were tempted to try." She reached out and covered Flora's hand with hers. "Thank you for telling me."

"I just wanted you to know you have a rocky path ahead of you if you want to be with him."

"I... I..."

Flora laughed and stood.

"No pressure. I'll just take this tray back to the kitchen. Then I'll ask Gladys to come and take a look at your ankle. I'm sure you'd rather not lay around in bed all day."

Flora disappeared before she had a chance to respond.

Did she want to be with him? *Oh, yes*, she thought, her eyes stinging. And it was much more than just the fiery physical attraction between them. She wanted to talk to him, make him smile, encourage him to show all the kindness he kept buried inside. But how was she going to convince him to trust her?

Flora came back a little while later, followed by Gladys. The witch checked the magic bandage, completely unharmed by the bath or her... activities in bed. She pronounced the healing well underway and allowed Elara to hobble to the living room.

The room was just as stunning as the bedroom with plastered walls, dark beams, and a huge stone fireplace. Both of the other women stayed for the rest of the day to keep her company. As she curled into the comfortable sofa and talked to them, she could easily imagine long winter nights snuggled up here with Grondar. Or sprawled out on the big rug in front of the fireplace as he showed her just how good those piercings would feel.

She was so lost in her fantasy that she didn't notice that both Flora and Gladys were staring at her with identical knowing looks.

"What?" she demanded.

"Nothing," Flora said, rising and smoothing a non-existent wrinkle out of her sweatsuit—bright pink today. "It's almost six. Grondar will be home soon so we're going to leave."

"Six is when the bakery closes," she protested. "You know he never leaves until eight or nine."

"Have you been watching him, dearie?" Gladys asked innocently, and she blushed.

"I'm pretty sure he'll be coming home early tonight," Flora said. "Come on, Gladys, we don't want to get in the way."

"In the way of what?"

But it was too late. The two women had already left. Great. She was going to be on her own for hours. But Flora was right—at precisely ten minutes after six, the door swung open and Grondar appeared. She gave him a grateful smile, but he closed his eyes, an odd look on his face.

"Time to go home," he announced.

CHAPTER 13

The look of betrayal on Elara's face made Grondar's chest ache. But the satisfaction he'd felt when he walked into his house and saw her smiling up at him had only confirmed his decision. The longer she stayed with him, the harder it would be to let her go. He wanted to believe that things could work out between them, but he was determined to take it slowly.

"Home?" she said slowly. "My ankle feels much better, but I'm not sure I can handle the stairs."

"I will carry you up and down whenever you ask. I just... This..."

She tilted her head, studying him, then nodded. To his relief, she didn't ask any more questions. Instead she pushed aside the blanket that had been covering her and rose a little unsteadily to her feet. He saw her wince as she put her weight on her ankle and immediately strode over and picked her up.

Fuck. Why did it always feel so right to have her in his arms?

She didn't object when he picked her up but she didn't smile at him the way she had the previous night. He looked away, afraid of what she might see in his eyes and finally noticed her clothing.

"What are you wearing?"

A hint of her usual humor appeared on her face. "It's hideous, isn't it? But Gladys brought it over for me so I didn't have a polite way to refuse."

Hideous was not the word he would have chosen. The material was a dull purple, a striking contrast to her creamy skin, but it wasn't the color that caught his attention, or the rather shape-less drape of the fabric.

"You didn't notice that it's transparent when the light hits it?" he growled.

"What?"

The fabric shifted as she moved, turning what had looked like solid fabric to little more than a layer of purple gauze, every detail of her luscious breasts clearly visible.

"Gladys gave me a see-through dress? And said it was one of her favorites?"

"Witches don't give a fuck about nudity, sugar."

She started to laugh, her breasts moving delightfully beneath the sheer fabric. He was torn between laughter and lust but settled for just pulling her closer.

"I'll get you a blanket," he promised as her laughter died away.

She studied him thoughtfully, then nodded.

"Probably just as well."

He found a soft blanket to wrap around her, and started to carry her out to his truck.

"I can walk, you know."

"No," he growled. He wasn't about to give up the opportunity to have her in his arms.

"Honestly. Gladys said it would be okay."

"Gladys also thought it was a good idea to dress you in a translucent gown. I'm not sure she can be trusted."

She laughed, her body vibrating against his.

"I just keep trying to picture her wearing this."

"It was probably only to travel back and forth to their meetings. You know that they go sky clad for most of their rituals, don't you?"

"Sky clad?"

"Naked. I stumbled across them one night when I was out late." He shuddered at the memory. "I think it scarred me for life."

He was placing her gently on the passenger seat as he spoke, their faces only inches apart.

"Is that why you wanted me to keep my underwear on?" she asked innocently. "Because you don't like naked women anymore?"

"You know damn well that there's one naked female I like very much," he growled.

Her mouth curved in a slow, seductive smile, and he almost kissed her. But if he kissed her now, he had no doubt that he'd end up carrying her back into his house and all his carefully laid plans would be for nothing. He clenched his hand on the door frame hard enough that the metal groaned, but somehow he found the strength to move back and close the door.

She didn't say anything on the short drive back to the bakery, but she still seemed thoughtful rather than angry or upset. Maybe he'd been wrong. Maybe she wanted to leave him? That thought annoyed him even more, and he was not in the best of moods when he pulled into the parking area behind the building. It must have shown on his face because she gave him a startled look when he lifted her out of the truck.

"Is anything wrong?"

"Not at all. Everything's fucking peachy."

If she wasn't bothered about leaving his house, he'd obviously done the right thing. He stomped up the stairs to her kitchen door, unlocked it, and stepped inside, kicking it shut behind him.

"Grondar, what is the matter with you?"

"I already told you it's nothing," he snarled.

"Fine. Since you so obviously don't want to be here, just put me down. If I can't make it up the stairs, I'll just sleep on one of the couches in the shop again."

"No."

She started to try and wiggle free, and he gave her ass a warning squeeze.

"What did I tell you about moving like that?"

"That you'd spank me. But that was when we were in your house. This is my house, and you don't get to be in charge."

He bent down and glared at her.

"I'm always in charge, sugar."

"Not in my house you're not."

Once again, their faces were only inches apart. Her eyes blazed, and her breasts rubbed deliciously against his chest as her breath came in rapid pants. He couldn't resist. He kissed her.

For a brief second, she didn't respond, but then she sighed against his mouth and kissed him back just as hungrily. She tasted as sweet as the last sun-ripened berries of summer, and he wondered how he'd managed to go an entire day without kissing her. Her kitchen table was the nearest horizontal surface, and he was carrying her towards it, intent on getting her naked as soon as possible, when he tasted a hint of copper. Most of the blood in his body had left his brain and gone straight to his cock so it took him a second to realize he was tasting blood. He immediately drew back and saw that one of his tusks had nicked the corner of her mouth.

"Oh, fuck. I'm so sorry, sugar."

She scowled at him. "Now you're sorry for kissing me?"

"Of course not, but I nicked your lip."

When she only looked confused, he gathered the drop of blood on his finger and showed it to her.

"You bit me? I didn't even notice."

She reached for him again, but the incident had reminded him that humans were not only inconsistent, they were also fragile. He picked her up again, carrying her as carefully as he would have carried a baby up the stairs to her apartment.

"I really don't know why you want to bring me up here. You know there's nothing—"

She stopped abruptly as he carried her into her living room.

"My furniture." She gave a delighted laugh. "I don't believe it. How did you get it here?"

"One of the delivery drivers is also an Other so I called in a favor."

And he was never going to hear the end of it, but it was worth it for the delighted look on her face.

He was not as pleased. The mid-century leather couch looked comfortable and stylish in front of the brick wall, along with the coffee table that had also been part of the order, but the room was still very far from furnished. *She would be more comfortable in my house.* Perhaps he should...

"Did he bring the rest of it as well?"

"Yes."

He carried her through into the bedroom. She had selected a sleek platform bed, a brass-framed floor mirror, and a long dresser, so this room looked slightly more furnished although it still lacked any personal touches.

"I'm glad I got a king-size bed, just in case I have any visitors."

He knew that she was being deliberately provocative, but it didn't stop him from growling.

"What visitors?"

She sighed.

"You, Grondar. You're the only one I want in my bed."

The provocative tone had vanished and he wanted so badly to believe her, but...

"Why do I suspect that this is where you tell me you need your space?" she asked when he didn't answer her.

"Yes. I mean, no. Yes."

"That was definitive. Why don't you put me down so we can discuss it?"

"Not on the bed."

He was quite sure that if they sat on the bed, talking would be the last thing they ended up doing.

"Well, now that I have some furniture, we could sit on the couch like civilized adults."

"I don't feel very civilized, sugar," he said, but he carried her back to the living room and sat down on the couch.

He had intended to put her down next to him but ended up keeping her on his lap instead. She didn't protest, simply looking at him expectantly as he tried to figure out how to explain.

"I am... possessive," he said at last. *Too possessive,* Gwendolyn had sneered. "The longer you stay in my house, the more I will want to keep you there."

"I wasn't in any hurry to leave," she said quietly.

"I know."

He didn't add anything else, and after a moment she sighed again.

"So you decided to bring me back home before you started getting possessive?"

How could he tell her it was already far too late for that? The very fact that she referred to this bare apartment as home made him want to growl.

She nodded, and slid off his lap to sit next to him.

"I suppose I'd better get used to being on my own again. Thank you for taking care of the furniture."

"It's not enough."

"No, but it's a beginning. I can build from that."

The words hung in the air between them before he cleared his throat.

"I stocked the refrigerator up here, but if there is something you would like me to bring you I'd be happy to do so."

"No thank you. It's been an... interesting twenty-four hours. I think I'll just have an early night."

He rose reluctantly to his feet fighting the urge to throw her over his shoulder and carry her back to his den—his house.

"Do not attempt the stairs on your own," he warned. "If you want to go up or down, you call me, do you understand?"

"Any time? Night or day?"

He knew she was trying to tease him, but it was clear her heart wasn't in it.

"Any time, sugar." He would always come if she needed him. "I'll be back in the morning."

"Why? To check on me?"

He allowed himself the pleasure of cupping the soft curve of her cheek.

"No, simply because I want to see you. I'm turning down the heat, not shutting off the oven."

She gave him a much more genuine smile.

"I think your baking metaphor leaves a little to be desired, but we'll see how far we can get with a cool oven. Good night, Grondar. And thank you again for the furniture."

"You're welcome, sugar."

He forced himself to turn and go back down the stairs, even though every step felt as if he were dragging his feet through quicksand. He made sure he locked the door behind him, but he didn't even consider going home. He went to the bakery instead. He might not be staying with her, but fuck if he was going to leave her alone and unprotected. He wandered aimlessly around the kitchen for a while, but for the first time in his life, the idea of baking didn't appeal to him.

"I must be insane," he muttered to himself.

He could be upstairs with her right now, trying out that stylish new bed instead of sitting alone in a dark kitchen. He kept finding himself heading for the door, but his reasoning hadn't changed. He needed time—and so did she.

He finally picked up one of the cookbooks in his collection, chose a recipe at random, and set to work.

Sunlight on Grondar's face woke him the next morning. He'd spent the night in his office chair, and he'd slept later than he intended. Perhaps that wasn't surprising since he'd been up most of the night, fighting the urge to join Elara. But now it was morning and he had promised her that he would come by in the morning.

He quickly brushed his teeth and washed his face, then headed next door. He was at the foot of the stairs to her apartment when he heard her laughing in the shop. Already annoyed that she had taken the stairs alone, he was even more pissed when he saw her standing by herself in the coffee shop talking to Eric, the delivery driver. Neither one of them noticed him.

"I can't thank you enough for delivering my furniture," she said with a warm smile. "I know the weather isn't the best at this time of year."

"No problem. I'm glad to be of service," Eric said. "I grew up here so I'm used to the roads. Besides, it gave me an opportunity to visit my family, and meet a delightful new resident."

Fucking bastard.

"I still appreciate it. Maybe I should name a coffee after you."

For some reason, that pushed him over the edge.

"Like hell you will. If you're going to name a coffee after anybody, it's going to be me."

He stomped behind the counter, glared at his so-called friend, and deliberately put his body between Elara and Eric, caging her against the rear counter.

"Grondar, what are you doing?"

She pushed ineffectually against his back but he ignored her, still focused on the male smirking at him from across the counter. Eric was the same troll who had tried to force him to eat swamp mud all those years ago. Their sizes had evened out over the years, although Eric always maintained he was taller and Grondar argued that the massive horns on the troll's head didn't count.

"I thought you were going back to Charlotte."

"I am, but while I'm here I thought I'd spend some time appreciating all the sights."

Eric tried to peer around the bulk of his body to look at Elara, and Grondar growled again. Eric held up his hands in mock surrender.

"Nice to meet you, Elara," he called. "I hope we can get better acquainted next time I'm in town."

Eric smirked at him again and sauntered out of the shop. As soon as the door closed behind him, Grondar stepped away from the counter, releasing Elara. She gave him the adorable glare that always turned him on.

"What the hell was that all about?"

"You came down the stairs by yourself," he growled.

She rolled her eyes.

"Yes, but honestly my ankle is just fine."

"Dressed like that," he added.

"What's wrong with what I'm wearing?"

She seemed genuinely confused as she looked down at her outfit. The dark turtleneck accentuated her lush breasts, and the flirty little pleated skirt over her dark tights was straight out of a schoolboy's dream. At least she had the sense to put on soft flat-heeled boots.

"And you were going to name a coffee after him," he roared.

"That's why you're upset?"

"You never offered to name one after me."

He knew how ridiculous he sounded, but he couldn't help it. Her hands went to her luscious hips as she did her best to look fierce.

"If I were going to name a coffee after you, I'd call it the Grumpy Orc."

"Grumpy?" he growled, taking a step towards her.

She didn't back down, even though he towered over her.

"Grumpy? You ain't seen nothing yet, sugar."

Before she could say anything, he picked her up and threw her over his shoulder the way he'd wanted to do since the very first moment he'd seen her. He clamped his hand down on her ass to keep her in place, wedging his thumb between those luscious cheeks, and headed for the stairs.

"Grondar, what are you doing? I thought you wanted space."

"Fuck space. I want you."

She stopped struggling. He carried her straight to the bedroom before letting her down.

"Take off your clothes," he ordered.

CHAPTER 14

*C*aveman—*no, cave* orc, *Grondar is the hottest yet,* Elara decided. All that growly possessiveness, not to mention being tossed over his huge shoulder, had her whole body humming with arousal. Not that that meant she intended to make this easy for him.

Given his history, she hadn't really been surprised that he felt the need to put some space between them. That didn't mean it didn't bother her, although she would have been a lot more upset about it if it weren't quite clear how much he hated it.

"What if I don't want to?" she asked provocatively.

"Then I hope you don't like that outfit very much, sugar."

Oh my. The thought of him ripping her clothes off was surprisingly appealing, but she was very fond of this skirt. She still couldn't resist issuing her own challenge.

"What if I want you to take your clothes off?"

He didn't bother answering her. He put one hand behind his head, grabbed the neck of his T-shirt and yanked it off with one hard tug, toed off his boots, and kicked off his jeans, leaving seven feet of magnificent, naked orc. Her mouth went dry as her clit pulsed with excitement.

"Okay," she whispered.

She was wearing more clothes, and she was nowhere near as good at stripping them off as he was, but he didn't complain. His eyes watched her hungrily, and his cock flexed each time she removed another garment. He stopped her when she was down to a silky red bra and matching thong.

"I want to remove those myself," he growled.

He kneeled in front of her, and even kneeling their faces were almost level as he put his big hands on her waist and pulled her closer. His mouth closed down on her breast, hot and wet and wonderful even through the silk, sucking hard enough that she clutched his shoulders to keep herself steady. When he switched to the other breast, the cool air against the wet silk only added to the sensations coursing through her. The whole time he worked her breasts, his hands moved over the rest of her body, skating down her back, teasing the sensitive area behind her knees, and returning over and over to her ass, squeezing her cheeks and letting his finger slide along the line of her thong. Everywhere he touched her added to her arousal but it wasn't quite enough to push her over the edge. She was shaking with need when he finally raised his head from her breasts.

"Time to remove this layer," he growled, releasing the catch on her bra and revealing her breasts to his avid gaze. "So fucking pretty."

He swiped his thumb across the stiff peaks, and her nails dug into his shoulders. She wouldn't have thought that the thin silk was much of a barrier, but the direct touch of skin against skin was even better.

"Do you want to come like this, sugar? With my mouth on these pretty sugar tits?"

"I want to come with you inside me."

His eyes darkened, and he rose to his feet, lifting her up with him and carrying her over to the bed. Given his apparent obsession with her ass, she expected him to put her on her stomach. Instead, he placed her on her back, his big body looming over her and blocking out everything except for him.

"I'll have to go slow," he muttered, and it almost sounded like he was talking to himself.

"Didn't you want to get rid of my panties first?"

"Not just yet."

His big hand stroked across the wet silk, and she shuddered.

"Two," he growled.

"Two what?"

"Two climaxes. To make sure you're ready to take me."

"I don't think that's—"

Before she could finish, he pressed his thumb firmly against her clit and that one touch was enough to trigger her climax. She could have sworn she saw stars, her body shaking as the convulsions raced through her.

"That's one," she gasped when she had enough breath to speak.

"I'm not sure that one counted. I barely even touched you."

His smile was wicked, and she couldn't help returning it.

"That one definitely counts," she assured him fervently. "In fact, I think that's more than enough to get me ready."

"Don't lie to me, sugar," he warned.

She rolled her eyes and lifted her legs to circle his waist, trying to draw him closer. The broad head of his cock pressed tantalizingly against the silk still covering her entrance. He shuddered, his hips jerking forward, her thin panties the only barrier between them. The pressure against the cloth also drew it tighter against her swollen clit and she moaned.

"Maybe you're ready after all," he growled, looking down at where their bodies were almost joined.

"God, yes."

"Slowly," he repeated, and slid her panties to one side.

He pushed, and she felt her body stretching, trying to open around that enormous girth. He pushed again. There was a brief, burning stretch as her body resisted and then gave way and he slid inside.

"Look how pretty you look taking my cock," he growled. "Ready for more?"

"Less talk, more cock," she gasped.

He grinned and obeyed, thrusting slowly deeper. Every time she started to wonder if she could take any more, one of his piercings would press against the perfect spot or the ridges of his tattoos would stroke the sensitive inside of her channel and she would take another inch. By the time he'd buried the entire thick length of his cock inside her, her whole body was quivering, muscles taut.

"Good girl," he whispered. "Now come for me, sugar."

He reached between their bodies and lightly pinched her fully exposed clit, and her world went up in flames. Her vision sheeted white as her body arched, her channel fluttering helplessly around the massive invader. He roared and started thrusting, each stroke prolonging her climax as his piercings slid across places inside her she'd never known existed. All she could do was cling to him until he roared again and she was filled with an endless rush of hot liquid.

He collapsed down on top of her, shuddering, his breath coming in harsh pants, but he managed not to crush her beneath him. Her own breathing was more than a little shaky as she ran her fingers through the long dark silk of his hair until he finally raised his head.

His face was completely relaxed, his eyes soft as he smiled at her.

"Are you all right, sugar?"

"I'm fantastic, although I think I'm going to have to buy some new windows."

"Windows?"

Was there anything cuter than the confused look on that rugged face?

"You roar. Loudly. I'd be willing to bet that Gladys is already on the phone to your grandmother."

He started to laugh, the vibration rippling through their joined bodies, and she gasped as her still swollen clit pulsed with excitement. His eyes darkened as his laughter died away.

"In that case, it's your turn, sugar."

His hips rocked against hers and her arousal started to build again.

"What do you mean?"

"I wouldn't want her to think you're being neglected. Your turn to roar."

"Women don't roar," she managed to say as he rolled them over so she was astride that huge orc cock.

His eyes gleamed as a big hand came up to cover her breast.

"You will, sugar."

He was right.

AFTER THE SECOND TIME, SHE WAS TOO EXHAUSTED TO move. Her eyes started to drift close as Grondar climbed out of bed and dressed, and she was almost asleep when he bent down to kiss her.

"I don't want to leave you, sugar, but I need to do some baking."

"Okay," she said, burrowing deeper into the pillows.

"Be sure and call me when you want to come downstairs."

She waved a noncommittal hand and he growled, but she chose to ignore him.

"Don't pretend you didn't hear me."

She smiled, but she kept her eyes closed. She heard him chuckle, and he brushed a last kiss across her cheek.

"Sleep well, sugar."

She did. She'd spent most of the previous night tossing and turning and thinking about Grondar. As a result, it was almost noon when she woke up again. She sighed and stretched, relishing the slight, lingering ache between her legs, and decided to take a quick shower before going to find Grondar.

She'd unpacked her boxes during one of her sleepless periods, and after her shower she hunted through her underwear drawer until she found a pretty white eyelet set, complete with little pink bows. Her ample curves turned it from innocent to provocative, and she suspected that Grondar would appreciate the contrast. A long blue dress with buttons down the front was next. *Easy access*, she thought as she opened the top buttons enough to provide a teasing hint of cleavage, her body already humming with excitement.

She hurried down the steps, then paused at the bottom to listen to Annie talking cheerfully to the customers in the coffee shop. Elara had met her earlier that morning after she'd made her cautious way downstairs. She was a compact female with short brown hair and a cheerful face, and Elara liked her on sight. Knowing that Flora also approved of the brownie, she didn't hesitate to ask Annie if she'd like the job on an ongoing basis. Annie accepted enthusiastically before she dashed off to take her daughter to school. She'd introduced Eric on her way out.

Since the coffee shop was in capable hands, she was free to go find her grouchy orc—although she seriously doubted he was grouchy right now. Her heart skipped a beat as she looked through his kitchen window and saw him talking to a stunningly beautiful dark-haired woman. Tall and slender enough to be a model, the woman was almost her exact opposite. What the hell was the stranger doing with her orc?

She opened the door in time to hear Grondar speak.

"What do you want, Gwendolyn?"

This was Gwendolyn? The one who had broken his heart? She'd be damned if she were going to let this woman hurt him again. She marched into the kitchen, ready for battle.

CHAPTER 15

Grondar very reluctantly left Elara to sleep and returned to the bakery. He hated to leave her, but he did have a business to run and customers who depended on him. He had the ridiculous urge to shout from the rooftops that she was his female, but he managed to keep it in check.

He also resisted the urge to grin at Ermengarde when he poked his head into the front room to let her know he was back. Apparently, his efforts were unsuccessful because she took one look at him and laughed.

"What?" he growled.

"Nothing. You just seem very... relaxed."

"Not too relaxed to fire impertinent help."

He couldn't even manage to fake a scowl, and she shook her head.

"Pitiful. Now go check the order sheet. The café wants four more loaves of that sourdough."

"I'll take a look."

He escaped back into the kitchen and set to work. As always, the familiar process soothed him, although thoughts of Elara kept intruding in the most pleasant way. He was scooping batter into a cupcake pan when he heard Ermengarde on the other side of the kitchen door.

"You can't go back there."

His assistant sounded unusually aggressive, but when the person she was talking to responded, he understood why.

"Oh, Grondar and I are old friends. I'm sure he won't mind."

Friends? Gwendolyn thought they had been friends? He'd spent a good deal of time thinking about it after their relationship ended and realized she'd never seemed particularly interested in just spending time with him. He'd certainly never laughed with her the way he did with Elara.

"If you'll wait here, I'll check and see if he's available," Ermengarde said coolly.

He heard the familiar sound of Gwendolyn's disapproving sniff, but the next person through the door was his assistant.

"Boss," she whispered. "You'll never guess who's here."

"Gwendolyn. I heard."

Apparently, she'd been listening at the door because as soon as she heard her name she came sweeping into the kitchen. Ermengarde shot him a quick look, but he just motioned her back to the front room.

"That's right. *C'est moi!*" Gwendolyn cried dramatically.

He bit back a sigh, studying her. She was both very familiar and very different. Her clothes looked elegant and expensive, and she'd cut her hair into a sleek bob that framed her angular features. She was tall for a human and she'd always been slender, but now she looked too thin, especially in contrast to Elara's delicious curves.

"Gwendolyn." He kept his voice as neutral as possible, but she looked taken aback. What had she expected? A welcoming committee? "What are you doing here?"

"Why, I came to see you, of course."

She took a step towards him and he took a matching step back, then slid his cupcake pan into the oven.

"Is that any way to treat an old friend?' she asked, pouting.

He'd been a slave to that pout once—now it barely registered. He raised an eyebrow.

"I'm not sure we were ever friends."

"Of course we were. That's why you were the first person I thought about."

He sighed. "What do you want, Gwendolyn?"

The door opened as he spoke and Elara came in, looking even more beautiful than she had when he left her. He was afraid she wouldn't be happy to see another woman in his kitchen, but she acted as if she didn't even see Gwendolyn. She walked straight to him and put her arms around his waist, tilting her head back for a kiss. Her hair was up in the high ponytail he loved, and he wrapped it around his hand as he kissed her.

As always, the world went away as soon as their lips met, and he actually forgot about Gwendolyn until he heard her speak.

"Aren't you going to introduce me to your... friend, Grondar?"

Her husky voice sounded unusually stiff, but Elara turned and gave her a sunny smile.

"Oh, I'm sorry. I didn't even see you there."

He hid a smile as Gwendolyn stiffened. He knew she wasn't used to being overlooked and she obviously didn't like it.

"And I'm a lot more than Grondar's friend," Elara continued. "Aren't I, pookie?"

Pookie? He barely managed to keep a straight face.

"That's right, sugar," he agreed as he tugged her back against his side.

"You two are together?"

Gwendolyn actually looked shocked. Did she really think he'd been pining for her all these years?

"Of course." Elara put her hand on his chest and smiled again. "What woman could resist all this?"

Another flash of surprise, then Gwendolyn shrugged dismissively.

"How nice for you." Ignoring Elara completely, she looked up at him and smiled. "I have the most exciting news."

"Oh?"

"I don't know if you're aware of it, but this little Winter Festival of yours has made quite a splash on social media. It was very clever of you, darling. Sheer marketing genius."

Elara's hand tightened at the endearment but she remained silent.

"I had nothing to do with it. It was Elara's idea."

Gwendolyn waved a dismissive hand.

"That doesn't matter. The point is that there's a lot of interest in mon—I mean, Others—right now. I've been approached by Taran Media about putting on a cooking show in Los Angeles. Doesn't that sound wonderful?"

Why was she telling him about it? Did she actually think he'd care? He shrugged.

"I suppose. If that's what you want."

"Not me, darling, *us*! I'll make all the arrangements and manage everything. All you have to do is show up and prepare some of your wonderful meals. It will be just like we planned back in school."

"You seem to have forgotten that the reason those plans fell through originally was because you took the internship and left with your human boyfriend."

She pouted again, but now he could see the calculation behind it.

"That was a terrible mistake. I was just young and foolish. Don't you remember how good it used to be between us?"

"No," he said bluntly. "Especially not now that I know what it's like to be with someone who actually cares about me."

Gwendolyn looked down her patrician nose at Elara.

"Some little hometown nobody? What does she have that I don't have?"

"I have Grondar," Elara said, stepping in front of him. "I suppose I should thank you for being foolish enough to throw him away. I'm never going to make that mistake."

A warm glow filled him at her words.

"I didn't throw him away," Gwendolyn sputtered. "He loves me."

"No, he doesn't. I know that because I love him and he loves me back, and neither one of us is the kind of despicable person who would cheat on someone they pretended to love."

His ex actually flinched and retreated when Elara stepped towards her.

"So get in whatever fancy car brought you here and get the hell out of our town." She smiled a sweet, artificial smile. "And if you're thinking of getting into bed with Taran Media you'd better have an ironclad contract and demand to get paid up front. They don't have a good reputation."

"How do you know?"

"Because I was Chief Marketing Officer for CreatorCon."

Gwendolyn's eyes widened.

"But... but..."

"Buh-bye," Elara said firmly. "Get the hell out of my town."

Gwendolyn tried one last pleading look in his direction, but he just jerked his thumb at the door. She glared at both of them and left, and he immediately forgot about her as he turned to his female.

"You love me?" he demanded.

Her cheeks turned pink.

"Well, yes. Although that wasn't exactly how I planned to tell you."

"Thank the gods," he growled, lifting her up onto his workbench and popping open the next button on her dress.

"I'm sorry I spoke for you too."

Another button, and she gasped as he ran his finger along the edge of the virginal white bra framing her luscious cleavage.

"You did?" he asked, trying to decide how long he could wait before ripping it off. He settled for pushing the cups back far enough to uncover her pretty nipples.

"When I said that you l-loved me too."

The hint of uncertainty in her voice caught his attention, and he looked up to find her biting her lip.

"Since the moment you tried to burn down my bakery."

Her eyes sparkled indignantly. "I didn't do any—"

He hushed her by kissing her until she melted against him, then smiled down into her flushed face.

"I love you, sugar."

"Good. Now you can go back to what you were doing."

"You mean this?"

He ripped open the rest of her dress, sending buttons flying.

"That's a good start," she said breathlessly.

He laid her back on the counter, admiring the way the open dress framed her creamy skin, her breasts spilling over the deceptively innocent white bra. The matching panties were just as pretty but they were in his way, and he tugged them off to reveal the golden curls framing her pretty little pussy. He parted the flushed folds and slid a big green finger into her tiny entrance. She gasped and arched against his hand.

"You're wiggling, sugar."

She gave him a challenging look.

"And I'm going to keep doing it until you make me come."

He growled and clamped his hand on her hip as he bent down, lashing at her clit with his tongue as he drove his finger in and out in a demanding rhythm. She cried out, writhing against his hand and mouth until her body convulsed and sweet liquid heat flooded his tongue.

He was opening the top button on his jeans when the door flew open and his grandmother rushed in. Elara squeaked, and he quickly wrapped her dress back around as he glared at his grandmother.

"What the hell are you doing back here?"

Her eyes sparkled.

"Trying to stop you from setting the building on fire."

She pointed at the oven behind him, and he finally noticed the smoke drifting from the vent. The cupcakes. He'd forgotten the fucking cupcakes.

He turned off the oven and turned to find Elara sitting up on the counter, her shoulders shaking with laughter.

"Now who's trying to burn down the building?" she giggled.

"Close the bakery, Gran," he ordered, never taking his eyes off his beautiful, tempting mate. "I have other plans for the day."

"Apparently," Gran said dryly as she left. "I'll spread the word."

He had no doubt she would, but he didn't care. All he cared about was the woman laughing up at him as he took her in his arms.

"You're a dangerous woman, sugar."

"I'm not the one trying to set the place on fire—either time." The laughter died away as she reached up and threaded her fingers through his hair. "But I would have done it if I'd known it would end up like this. I love you, Grondar."

"I'd burn the building to the ground if it meant I could have you," he said hoarsely. "I love you too."

"Fortunately, arson isn't a requirement for love." She unwrapped the dress enough to reveal her still exposed breasts. "Why don't we go back to my apartment and create a different type of heat?"

He had no doubt they'd generate enough heat to keep him warm for the rest of his life.

EPILOGUE

 *ne month later...*

"I brought the balloons," Flora called to Elara as she entered their house.

Technically, it was still Grondar's house, but they spent almost every night here and they'd already agreed to rent out her apartment.

"Thanks for bringing them over."

Flora grinned at her. She was wearing a hot pink sweatsuit today in honor of Valentine's Day with Hot Stuff spelled out across the front in rhinestones.

"Nice outfit," Elara said.

"I can't wait to show Grondar. He's so cute when he's trying not to look disapproving." Flora's eyes widened as she looked around the living room. "You really went all out to celebrate, didn't you?"

She laughed. "You should see the bedroom."

"I'd rather not."

As the two of them sat on the couch, she followed Flora's gaze around the room. Flowers and candles covered almost every surface. She'd added cushions of red silk and pink velvet to the couch, as well as two huge quilted velvet floor cushions in front of the fireplace.

"Grondar appreciates girly things." Especially on her—her already extensive underwear collection was growing almost daily. "And he's been working so hard, he deserves it."

He'd been working overtime for the past week fulfilling all the special orders for Valentine's Day.

"You've been working hard as well, dear."

She had—the influx of new tourists had been wonderful for the coffee shop. She'd been so busy that she'd had to hire a second assistant, but she'd left the shop in their hands this afternoon while she came home to prepare.

"I know. I'm glad we're going to be closed for the next week."

They were closing so that the contractor could open up the wall between the bakery and the coffee shop, combining them into one operation.

"You both deserve a break," Flora agreed. She reached over and took Elara's hand. "Thank you," she said softly.

"For what?"

"For making my grandson smile again. For making him believe in love."

Her eyes filled with tears as she squeezed Flora's hand.

"He did the same for me."

"I know, but as soon as we talked for the first time, I knew you were the right one for him."

"Is that why you agreed to sell me the shop?"

"It was the Council's decision, not mine," Flora said piously, then grinned. "Although I may have nudged them in that direction."

"Because you wanted me for Grondar?"

Dark eyes twinkled at her. "Not entirely. We loved your plans for the coffee shop, and your ideas for the town. But the fact that I thought you'd be perfect for him certainly didn't hurt."

She started to laugh. "I suppose I should have guessed. Just please tell me you didn't use Gladys to get me here."

"Of course not."

Flora assumed her best butter wouldn't melt in her mouth expression, but Elara wasn't entirely convinced. Still, did it really matter? The important thing was that she was here and she and Grondar had found each other.

"I'm glad I came," she said softly.

Flora squeezed her hand, then jumped to her feet.

"I have to dash. I have to persuade Gladys to attend the dance tonight."

"Why?"

The old woman winked. "Because a certain handsome witch doctor will also be attending."

She laughed. "You're quite the matchmaker, aren't you?"

"It runs in my family, but I do think I have a knack for it," Flora said modestly. "And there are a lot of people in Fairhaven Falls who could use my help."

As she accompanied Flora to the door, she could only hope that the other woman was as successful for others as she had been for her. As soon as the door closed, she hurried to make the rest of her preparations.

An hour later, she heard the door open.

"I'm in the kitchen," she called.

"That sounds dangerous," he muttered as he came to join her, and she laughed.

He'd made several attempts to teach her a few simple recipes, but something always seemed to go wrong. They usually ended up spending their time in the kitchen on more... interesting activities. Kitchen utensils were surprisingly versatile.

He smiled at her as he entered the kitchen, just as he always did, but she could tell how tired he was—it took him a full second before he finally realized what she was wearing. His eyes gleamed as he prowled towards her.

"You're wearing that apron," he growled.

It was the same white apron with the lacy ruffle around the bib and the flirty little skirt that she'd worn at the Winter Festival.

The difference this time was that she wasn't wearing anything beneath it except a pair of sheer white panties. The hem brushed the top of her thighs, and her breasts threatened to peek out from behind the bib every time she moved. She twirled teasingly in front of him.

"Do you approve, pookie?"

"Do you have to call me that ridiculous name?" he grumbled, but she knew it amused him.

"It's no more ridiculous than sugar."

"But I call you sugar because you taste so sweet. Where the hell does pookie come from?"

"Maybe it's because you like to 'pook' me with that big old cock of yours."

"I can't argue with that." He put a big hand on her arm and tugged her closer. "In fact, I think I'm ready for a little 'pooking' right now."

"You're not too tired?" she asked, studying his face.

"I'm never too tired for you, sugar."

He certainly did seem to have an endless supply of energy where she was concerned.

"Good. But sit down for a minute first. I have a couple of Valentine surprises for you."

He grumbled again, but sat at the kitchen table as she handed him a mug.

"Here, try this."

He gave it a suspicious glance.

"What is it?"

"It's just coffee. One of my experiments."

He took a cautious step, then smiled.

"I like it. A little bitter to start off with, but then you catch the sweetness behind it. What do you call it?"

"A Grumpy Orc, of course." He laughed, but she could see the pleasure on his face. "I told you I'd name a coffee after you."

"I think this one's a winner."

"Just like you."

He finished the coffee in two big swallows, and pulled her down on his knee, sliding his hand beneath the bib of the apron to cup her breast and tug teasingly at her nipple.

"I told you this apron gave a male ideas, and I have plenty of them right now."

"Not yet." She let her hand trail down over his magnificent chest and lower, running her fingernails lightly over the denim covering his cock. "I have a few ideas of my own. Do you remember saying something about flipping up the skirt as you bent me over the cooler?"

His cock flexed against her hand and she smiled.

"Is this what you had in mind?"

She slipped free of his hands and went to the far side of the kitchen, pulling off a tablecloth to reveal the industrial cooler she'd had delivered earlier. It was exactly the same as the one that had been in her stall that evening.

Smiling at him, she bent over the cooler, knowing the apron would frame her ass perfectly. The cool metal felt wonderful against her aching nipples, and dampness already coated her thighs. She looked back over her shoulder and saw him staring at her, his knuckles white as he gripped the table.

"Happy Valentine's Day, pookie," she whispered and wiggled her ass at him.

Her words seemed to release him. He growled and rose to his feet, looming even larger than usual as he stalked across the kitchen towards her. He opened his jeans as he came, fisting his huge cock in a meaty hand.

"Is this what you want, sugar? My big cock in your pretty little pussy?"

"God, yes."

He didn't bother with any fancy maneuvers with her panties this time. He simply ripped them off of her and plunged home in one long hard stroke.

Holy crap! She clung to the cooler, panting, as her body struggled to handle the overwhelming stretch. As excited as she was, he was a lot to take. He didn't try and hurry her, just kept her speared on his cock as he waited for her body to adjust. His hands settled over her ass, massaging gently. When he stopped, she wiggled against his hand and he growled.

"Are you asking me to spank this luscious ass of yours, sugar? Because if you do that again I will."

She deliberately wiggled again, and his hand descended, creating the delicious sting she'd come to crave. It was even better this way—the shock reverberating through their combined bodies and making his piercings vibrate inside her channel. He did it again, leaving her ass warm and glowing, then slid his thumb between her cheeks. She quivered in anticipation, already knowing what he was about to do. He started to move, gliding slowly in and out of her pussy as he circled the delicate rosette, awakening all the sensitive nerves.

"You look so pretty like this, sugar. Stretched open around my cock, asking me to fill you completely."

He slid his thumb into her ass, the additional thickness pressing against her already overstuffed channel. She clutched the cooler desperately, already on the verge of climax.

"That's my good girl," he growled, and started to thrust.

He wasn't gentle. He fucked her hard and fast, and she loved every minute. Her climax roared over her with his third thrust, but he didn't even pause, his hips pistoning against her as he pressed his thumb deeper into her ass, the pressure dragging the ridges of his tattoos across her sensitive flesh with each stroke. She rolled from one climax straight into another until at last he roared and pulled her against him, burying himself an impossible inch deeper as his seed flooded her insides, the hot rush of liquid sending her into one final shaky climax.

He covered her with his body, holding her until their breathing steadied, then reluctantly withdrew. He went to the sink and returned with a warm wet cloth, washing her gently before lifting her into his arms. He carried her into the living room and sat down in the big chair with her on his lap. She sighed happily and snuggled against him.

"That wasn't too rough, was it, sugar?"

"Not at all. You know I love it." She smiled up at him. "You know I love you."

"I love you too, and I thank the gods every day for bringing you to me."

"You might want to include your grandmother in those prayers," she said dryly. "She told me today that's why she encouraged the Council to hire me."

He shook his head and laughed. "I'm not really surprised."

"You're still dressed," she suddenly noticed.

"I didn't have time to take my clothes off, not when your pretty little pussy needed me." He smiled when she blushed. "As it turns out, it's very convenient. It means I don't have to go anywhere to get this."

He reached into his shirt pocket and pulled out a ring box. Her heart started to beat triple time as he opened it to reveal a beautiful diamond ring, with a central solitaire and smaller diamonds swirling up next to it. She traced the stylized lines with her finger.

"Are those flames?"

"I thought it was appropriate since it was a fire that brought us together in the first place." He gave her an anxious look. "Do you like it?"

"I love it."

"And will you marry me?"

"Yes!" she cried, flinging her arms around him so enthusiastically that he rocked backwards.

"Thank the gods," he whispered, and kissed her.

. . .

Across town, Flora smiled as she felt the final threads of Grondar and Elara's connection snap together. She'd never made a more satisfying match.

As she waited for Gladys outside the big barn decorated for the Valentine's dance, she studied the people entering. Who was going to be next?

AUTHOR'S NOTE

Thank you so much for reading **Cupcakes for My Orc Enemy**! I have so much fun with these cozy monster romances! I love my grumpy, dirty-talking orc and his feisty match - and I hope you do too!

Whether you enjoyed the story or not, it would mean the world to me if you left an honest review on Amazon – reviews are one of the best ways to help other readers find my books!

Thank you all for supporting these books - I couldn't do it without you!

And, as always, a special thanks to my beta team – Janet S, Nancy V, and Kitty S. Your thoughts and comments are incredibly helpful!

Next up - we return to Fairhaven Falls in **Trouble for My Troll**!

Will has no intention of remaining in Fairhaven Falls, which means that the curvy little female who collides with him - literally - can't be more than a distraction. So why does his inner troll want to carry her off to his den and keep her forever? He doesn't even have a den!

Trouble for My Troll is available on Amazon!

Ready for another cozy monster romance? Then you'll love **Extra Virgin Gargoyle**!

When Angie accepts a part-time job cataloging the library of the vast Gothic mansion on the edge of town, the brooding gargoyle owner turns out to be even more fascinating than his collection.

Can a curvy librarian tame a grumpy gargoyle?

Extra Virgin Gargoyle is available on Amazon!

And don't miss these other Sweet Monster Treats!

The Single Mom and the Orc by me!
Candy for My Orc Boss by Ava Ross
Single Orc Dad by Ava Ross
Cookies for My Orc Neighbor by Michele Mills
Twins for the Wild Orc by Michele Mills

To make sure you don't miss out on any new releases, please visit my website and sign up for my newsletter!

www.honeyphillips.com

OTHER TITLES

COZY MONSTERS

Fairhaven Falls

Cupcakes for My Orc Enemy

Trouble for My Troll

Fireworks for My Dragon Boss

The Single Mom and the Orc

Monster Between the Sheets

Extra Virgin Gargoyle

Without a Stitch

HOMESTEAD WORLDS

Seven Brides for Seven Alien Brothers

Artek

Benjar

Callum

Drakkar

Endark

Frantor

Gilmat

You Got Alien Trouble!

Cosmic Fairy Tales

Jackie and the Giant

Blind Date with an Alien

Her Alien Farmhand

KAISARIAN EMPIRE

The Alien Abduction Series

Anna and the Alien

Beth and the Barbarian

Cam and the Conqueror

Deb and the Demon

Ella and the Emperor

Faith and the Fighter

Greta and the Gargoyle

Hanna and the Hitman

Izzie and the Icebeast

Joan and the Juggernaut

Kate and the Kraken

Lily and the Lion

Mary and the Minotaur

Nancy and the Naga

Olivia and the Orc

Pandora and the Prisoner

Quinn and the Queller

Rita and the Raider

Sara and the Spymaster

Tammy and the Traitor

Stranded with an Alien

Sinta - A SciFi Holiday Tail

Folsom Planet Blues

Alien Most Wanted: Caged Beast

Alien Most Wanted: Prison Mate

Alien Most Wanted: Mastermind

Alien Most Wanted: Unchained

Treasured by the Alien

Mama and the Alien Warrior

A Son for the Alien Warrior

Daughter of the Alien Warrior

A Family for the Alien Warrior

The Nanny and the Alien Warrior

A Home for the Alien Warrior

A Gift for the Alien Warrior

A Treasure for the Alien Warrior

Three Babies and the Alien Warrior

Cyborgs on Mars

High Plains Cyborg

The Good, the Bad, and the Cyborg

A Fistful of Cyborg

A Few Cyborgs More

The Magnificent Cyborg

The Outlaw Cyborg

The Cyborg with No Name

ABOUT THE AUTHOR

USA Today bestselling author Honey Phillips writes steamy science fiction stories about hot alien warriors and the human women they can't resist. From abductions to invasions, the ride might be rough, but the end always satisfies.

Honey wrote and illustrated her first book at the tender age of five. Her writing has improved since then. Her drawing skills, unfortunately, have not. She loves writing, reading, traveling, cooking, and drinking champagne - not necessarily in that order.

Honey loves to hear from her wonderful readers! You can stalk her at any of the following locations...

www.facebook.com/HoneyPhillipsAuthor
www.bookbub.com/authors/honey-phillips
www.instagram.com/HoneyPhillipsAuthor
www.honeyphillips.com

Printed in Great Britain
by Amazon

45935146R00088